NEVER BEEN KISSED

"How horrid he was!" Marianna exclaimed. "I shall not endure being kissed a second time, I assure you!"

She felt Rick's body go rigid against hers, and after a moment he said, rather incredulously, "A second time? Are you telling me you had your first kiss just now from John Bagwell? You have never been kissed before?"

"Never, and I daresay if all kisses are the same as the one I was just made to suffer, I heartily hope I shall never be kissed again!"

There was a moment of silence; then, astonishingly, she heard him laugh softly. He tightened his arms about her, pressing her against him, until she could feel the rumbling vibration of his laughter through his chest.

"Marianna, if you were kissed correctly, believe me, you would want to be kissed again."

"I don't believe it. Kissing is a horrid business! I shall never be kissed again!"

"Are you sure, Marianna?" he murmured. "You should be very certain before you make any rash judgments."

There was something rather tantalizing in his tone, and she looked up at him. Their eyes met, and when she suddenly realized that his handsome face was slowly nearing hers, she was powerless to do anything about it. Then he lowered his head and claimed her lips in a long, sensual caress.

Rick was right, Marianna thought dazedly. Kisses were like heaven when they were given correctly. . . .

Books by Nancy Lawrence

DELIGHTFUL DECEPTION
A SCANDALOUS SEASON
ONCE UPON A CHRISTMAS
A NOBLE ROGUE
MISS HAMILTON'S HERO
AN INTIMATE ARRANGEMENT

Published by Zebra Books

AN
INTIMATE
ARRANGEMENT

Nancy Lawrence

Zebra Books
Kensington Publishing Corp.
http://www.zebrabooks.com

ZEBRA BOOKS are published by

Kensington Publishing Corp.
850 Third Avenue
New York, NY 10022

Zebra and the Z logo Reg. U.S. Pat. & TM Off.

First Printing: September, 2000
10 9 8 7 6 5 4 3 2 1

Printed in the United States of America

Prologue

Mr. John Bagwell, the most esteemed solicitor in all of Hampshire, looked across his office at the two old men who sat eyeing each other with naked hostility. Had Mr. Bagwell not been acquainted with both of the elderly gentlemen for most of his life, he still would have known Cecil and Arthur Madison for brothers. They bore a striking physical resemblance: both lean with age, faces drawn, cheekbones showing in high relief. They even glared at each other in the same manner.

At last Cecil Madison broke the long silence. He brought his frail, thin hand down on the arm of his chair with a sharp snap that made Mr. Bagwell jump.

"I won't stand for this, do you hear? I won't stand for it!"

Arthur Madison watched his brother's momentary display of temper with a good deal of satisfaction. "You have no choice in the matter. Seven Hills belongs to me, and I have decided to sell it. The deal is struck."

"Seven Hills isn't yours to sell," countered Cecil as an angry rush of color tinted his pale face. "I hold the title to Seven Hills and always have. The place is mine."

"You mistake. Tell him, Bagwell."

Mr. Bagwell was unaccustomed to finding himself spoken to in such a way. Rather, he was used to being

treated with a good deal of deference and respect; but
he had been Arthur Madison's solicitor for some years,
and history had taught him that his client was not a
man given to pleasantries. Like his brother, Cecil, Arthur Madison was a man who spoke his mind. And, like
Cecil, Arthur often delighted in causing discomfort to
others. In fact, in Mr. Bagwell's opinion, the Madison
brothers were so much alike, from their cantankerous
tempers right down to the size of their fortunes, they
should have been the best of friends. Instead, they had
been at dagger drawing for decades, and they held each
other in the greatest aversion.

This was not the first time John Bagwell had found
himself up to his starched shirt points in the Madison
brothers' arguments. He was astute enough to realize that
their dispute over the little estate called Seven Hills was
simply the latest in a long line of volleys Arthur Madison
had launched over his brother's bow. He waited, expecting
Cecil Madison to counter with an attack of his own, as
was his usual style. Cecil simply glared at his brother.

Mr. Bagwell cleared his throat in a rather Solomon-like
manner. "Mr. Cecil, your brother holds the title to Seven
Hills, and he has elected to sell the property to a young
man just returned from the war. I assure you, the trans-
action is in good order. I handled the sale myself."

"I wouldn't care if the man in the moon handled it!"
spat Cecil. "Seven Hills is mine! Mine! And I've got the
proof right here!"

He reached into a coat pocket and withdrew a sheaf
of papers, yellowed with age and frayed along the creases
where they had been folded, then opened, then folded
again over countless years. He jabbed the papers in Mr.
Bagwell's direction. "You'll find these are in order, and
you'll find, too, that they prove that *he* doesn't own a
blade of grass at Seven Hills, much less the entire estate."

He graciously gave the solicitor a moment to scan the sheets of paper, then said, a bit triumphantly, "There! Don't those papers prove what I say? Well, don't they?"

Mr. Bagwell frowned. "They do appear to be in order, but—"

"There! Just as I said!" Cecil Madison pointed one long, arthritic finger at his brother. "I want that man arrested! I want him arrested for forgery and fraud and—and—!"

"There will be no arrests made in this office, Mr. Cecil," said John Bagwell with authority. "As a matter of fact, there will be no disposition to this property dispute until I have examined these papers thoroughly."

"Then, you'd best be quick about it," recommended Cecil, "for I have already bequeathed the property away."

Mr. Bagwell sat back in his chair, realizing that the counterattack he had expected had been launched. He had now only to await Mr. Arthur's reaction.

Arthur Madison obliged him. His pale face grew two patches of crimson, and he eyed his brother angrily. "What do you mean, you've bequeathed Seven Hills away, you damnable upstart? That property is mine!"

Cecil gave his gray head a slow, deliberate shake. "You mistake. Seven Hills belongs to me as I have always said, and I may do with the place as I please. And it pleases me to make a gift of it to a great-niece who has fallen on hard times."

"Make a gift of it?" repeated Arthur Madison with a snort of suspicion. "You've never made a gift in all your miserable, miserly years. You've done this just to spite me."

"And to spite me, you're trying to sell the place like a Turkish peddler right from under my nose!"

"Liar!"

"Thief!"

"Gentlemen, enough!" begged Mr. Bagwell. "We will settle this matter in a civil fashion."

The brothers glared at him in unabashed anger, their mouths pressed into tight little lines, their eyes bright and as hard as agates.

"Then, settle it, man!" commanded Arthur.

"You won't have an answer from me today," said Mr. Bagwell. He stood, hoping the feuding brothers would take the hint and realize that their meeting was at an end. "I will examine your papers, Mr. Cecil, and I will examine the law. Mark me, I shall make no determination until I am certain of the circumstances."

"And just how much time do you propose to take?" demanded Cecil irritably.

"As long as need be. Days. Perhaps weeks."

"But I've already sold the property," complained Arthur.

"And I've already given it away," countered Cecil.

"As of this moment, neither of you have the right to do either. But not to worry, for I am prepared to assist you in this. Mr. Arthur—with your permission, of course!—I shall contact the gentleman to whom you sold the property. And Mr. Cecil—if you will provide me her name and direction—I shall write to the great-niece to whom you gifted the estate. I shall simply explain to both parties that their ownership of Seven Hills is in question and instruct them both that they are not to take possession of the property until the matter is settled."

Arthur Madison scowled. "I don't like it. I don't like it one bit."

"Everything shall be resolved presently," Mr. Bagwell said, with assurance. In fact, he was of the opinion that the dispute would be settled rather soon. Past dealings with the Madison brothers told him that neither brother was averse to stretching the truth a bit if it would result in raising the other brother's hackles.

He was deeply suspicious of old Cecil Madison's story. Mr. Cecil had never before shown the least interest in Seven Hills, he had never before in his life made a gift of anything to anyone, and he had never once mentioned the existence of a great-niece. The great-niece was no doubt simply a product of Cecil's imagination, conjured in the heat of the moment just to thrust a spoke in Arthur's wheel. She probably didn't even exist.

He prayed she didn't exist.

One

Sitting on the rough bench seat beside the cart driver, Marianna Madison did her best to appear calm and composed. She touched one gloved hand to the back of her hair, just to assure herself that her black curls were still neatly tucked under the brim of her plain bonnet, and she forced herself to keep her gray eyes focused on the road ahead. It was all she could do to maintain her ladylike pose and keep from craning her neck to catch her first glimpse of the place she would call home.

Behind her, standing up in the back of the cart, her young brother, Robin, was chattering in excited accents, pointing out landmarks, and marveling over the size of the rolling hills through which they traveled. Their elderly nurse, Miss Blessington, was seated farther back on the bed of the cart, nestled between the boxes and bundles and trunks that comprised the sum total of their worldly possessions.

Marianna cast a glance at the cart driver and asked politely, "How much farther must we travel before we reach Seven Hills, Mr. Hendrick?"

The cart driver cleared his throat. "Just a piece of the road, miss, there's a hind dog leg, then along another piece, and there's Seven Hills."

He might as well have said the place was on the moon,

thought Marianna, with a small shake of her head. "A hind dog leg?" she repeated.

"He means a crooked path," said Robin helpfully, from his stance behind the bench. Just as Marianna began to wonder how a ten-year-old boy from an excellent family should come to know such cant, Robin gave a shout.

"There it is!" he cried, hopping unsteadily about on the jostling cart. "I see the rooftops. Marianna, wait till you see it—Seven Hills is a castle!"

Mr. Hendrick guided the creaking old cart off the road and up the crooked lane. They passed through a grove of trees and emerged to a stunning view of a sprawling home, of three—perhaps four—stories, set atop a green rolling hill. It was late in the day, and the glow from the setting sun glittered off the tall, many-paned windows that lined the facade of the house. The structure was built of rose red brick with white pediments atop the windows, and a plethora of chimneys jutted from its roof. The wide door was painted white, and a healthy ivy gracefully surrounded the door like welcoming arms.

"It's beautiful!" she murmured, a bit stunned. "Mr. Hendrick, are you certain this is Seven Hills?"

He gave a short nod. "Aye, miss, 'tis none other."

"I can scarce believe it," she said, in a wondrous tone. "I had thought a cottage—a small house, perhaps, but—but this! I never dreamed Seven Hills was so grand."

"Ah, miss, I hate to see ye get yer hopes up until ye've had a look at the place," said Mr. Hendrick kindly. "Seven Hills ain't been lived in for many a year, and it's been molderin' on its own. Ye might find yerself livin' in the best end of the pig trough, if ye get my meaning."

She didn't get his meaning at all, but she wasn't about to say so, for she didn't want any bad news or ill feelings to intrude upon the moment.

Mr. Hendrick had barely brought the old cart to a halt

at the door before Robin leapt over the side. He was up the few steps and through the door in an instant and disappeared for a moment or two inside the house before reappearing and exclaiming once again that the place was nothing short of a castle.

"Yes, dear, but you mustn't run off, for there is much to be done before night falls," said Marianna, as Mr. Hendrick solicitously helped her down. "We shall start, I suppose, by unloading our things from the cart."

"Rather, you shall start by unloading me," said their elderly nurse, as she slowly got to her feet and worked the kinks from her joints. "One more mile in this cart and I fear my teeth might have rattled right out of my head!"

"Poor Blessing," said Marianna, with sympathy, "was it too uncomfortable for you?"

"It wasn't a drive in the park, but there was nothing for it but to be left behind," said Miss Blessington philosophically. "Master Robin, you might show me a bit of the manners you've been taught and help me down."

In the end it took the assistance of Robin, Marianna, and the cart driver to ease Miss Blessington down to the ground. "There!" she exclaimed, after Marianna helped disentangle the woman's shawls from where they had snagged on a particularly rough section of the wooden cart. "I'm as glad as can be to set my feet back on the ground. I didn't relish traveling as another bit of baggage in the back, I assure you."

"It was horrid for you, I know, but there was no other way, dear Blessing," said Marianna soothingly. "Here, let me help you into the house, and we shall find a nice spot for you to rest."

"No need. I dare say I'm not any the worse for wear, for all the discomfort of that horrid old cart. There's work to be done, after all. I'll see to the kitchens if you like,

Miss Marianna. You men," she said with a pointed look at Robin, "shall unload the cart."

"Indeed we shall!" said Robin, swelling visibly at hearing himself referred to in such masculine terms. As Marianna busied herself with toting the lighter bandboxes and parcels into the house, Robin helped Mr. Hendrick carry the heavy crates and trunks. At least, he attempted to help, but as he made a great show of helping Mr. Hendrick carry a particularly heavy item up the steps of the great house, Marianna deeply suspected that the cart driver bore the majority of the weight.

"There's a strong lad," said Mr. Hendrick, in such a sincere fashion that Marianna felt certain he must have raised a brood of his own boys. "Watch yer step, there, and push off a bit the other direction. There's a lad."

They set the trunk down in the entry hall, and Robin dashed back out the door, eager to display his strength and carry the next item into the house.

"Thank you for being patient with my brother, Mr. Hendrick," said Marianna. "You will tell me, won't you, if he is more hindrance than help?"

"He's a fine lad, miss. Not very strong, but he's got good bottom."

She took that as a compliment and followed Mr. Hendrick back outside. They continued to work, unloading the old cart item by item and depositing their possessions in the entry hall. It was tiring work, and Marianna was glad to lift the last parcel from the back of the cart. Thankfully, it weighed very little, and she was able to carry it up the steps of her new home and set it carefully among the rest of the boxes, bags, valises, and bundles that had already accumulated along one side of the spacious entry hall.

She turned and cast a weary smile at Robin and the cart driver. "That's the last of it, thank goodness!"

Her brother let out a whoop. "I'm off to the stables!" he cried, and he made a dash for the still-open door.

"Just a moment, Robin," said Marianna with an authority that brought his escape up short. "The day is gone—it's almost dark—and I won't have you running off in a strange place we've never been before. You could be lost or wander away—"

"I'm never lost!" he said scornfully. "Besides, I'm only meaning to go to the stables. We saw them as we drove up the lane, and they're very nearby. Why, you have only to step outside and call to me if you wish me to return, and I'll come running."

Marianna hesitated, debating the wisdom of allowing her ten-year-old brother this bit of freedom. Certainly, he must be as exhausted as she from a day spent traveling over rough and troublesome roads. Surely, he must be anxious for his dinner and bed.

She was on the verge of insisting that he wait until morning when she saw the rather pleading look in his eye. "Please? I've been a pattern card the entire journey! I haven't wiggled or complained in the coach or fidgeted about to give you a headache. And I ate every bit of that horrid tea we had in the last village we passed through. Why, I even helped Mr. Hendrick unload all the luggage from the back of the cart without so much as a whimper. *Please?*"

He was right; Robin had been on his best behavior for the past week. Obedient, helpful—Marianna suspected that he considered such behavior his way of helping during a most difficult time. The decision she had made to uproot her little family and move to Newmarket had been a particularly agonizing one. Orchestrating the move had been stressful. They had journeyed to a place they had never seen before, and with every passing mile she had berated herself over the wisdom of her decision. Through it all, Robin had been a golden child, and even Miss Blessington had softened her usually gruff mien to offer, with heartfelt sincerity, to ease Marianna's burden a little by making her home in a different direction.

"These are difficult times, Miss Marianna," she had said, "and you've got a load to carry, what with providing for your brother and all. I shouldn't want to be the one to inflict any more burden on you."

Marianna had stared at her. "You're—you're not thinking of leaving, are you? But, where will you go?"

"No place in particular. Just stand me out by the side of the road, and don't give me another thought."

"Don't be silly!" she had exclaimed, with a slight laugh of relief. "You know very well Robin and I could not go on without you. Why, you've been with our family for years."

"I served your mother and father for years, God rest their souls, and I rather thought I'd be on their pension in my later life. I never intended that I should be added to your responsibilities—not now when you're carrying the weight of the world on those shoulders of yours."

"I'm carrying nothing of the kind," Marianna had responded with certainty, "and I won't have you speaking as though you were some sort of burden to me. On the contrary, you know I rely upon you to help care for Robin, and you also know how hopeless I am in the kitchen. Why, were it not for you, we might have starved by now."

"Not starved," Miss Blessington had said, with a sniff, "but you might have been forced to eat some very nasty and unappetizing meals."

Marianna had laughed, and in the end she succeeded in allaying Miss Blessington's fears. She would never have considered her old nurse a burden to be discarded, especially now when Marianna needed her more than ever. She needed her to lend a willing ear, to tell her that the decisions she was making were right, to help deal with the troubles of the world. Most of all, Marianna needed her to help with Robin, who stood awaiting her answer with an expression of angelic pleading on his young face.

"Very well, you may go to the stables—" No sooner did the words leave her lips, than Robin let out a whoop and cry and dashed out the door.

She meant to say more, but refrained from calling him back. Instead, she turned toward Mr. Hendrick and thanked him kindly for the use of his cart in transporting them from the village that had been the last stop in their journey to their new home.

"You cannot know how much I appreciate your help, for without you, I cannot think how we might have managed."

She dipped her slender fingers into her reticule and grasped the last precious coins that remained, but he stopped her, saying, "Never you mind that, miss, for I couldn't take any lolly from you. Not now, after seeing your situation, so to speak."

"But we agreed upon a price, Mr. Hendrick. I couldn't possibly take advantage of your kindness and not keep my part of the bargain we struck back in the village."

He shook his head resolutely. " 'Twouldn't be right, miss."

"But I insist. I won't be a charity case, I assure you!"

"No. 'Twouldn't be right," he said again, and for emphasis, he turned and walked purposefully toward the door. He threw the door open and looked back at her. His expression turned thoughtful. "Is there just the three of ye, then? Ye, the boy, and the old woman?"

"Why, yes. But if you are thinking Seven Hills is much too large a home for my brother and nurse and me, I assure you, we shall revel in having so much room to ramble in. Our old home, you see, was nothing but a two-room cottage, and we were very cramped, I'm afraid."

He nodded, but still he hesitated by the door. "And there don't be a husband or an uncle? Someone to look after ye?"

A number of possible replies flitted across Marianna's mind, and for a moment she didn't know whether to be offended or warmed that the rough old cart driver would show such concern. At last she smiled slightly. "We manage very well for ourselves, thank you."

"I should warn ye that nights here come as black as a Newgate knocker, miss, and the wind do howl. Why do ye not let me take ye back to the village? There be room there for ye, and I'll drive ye back out here come the morning."

"Thank you, Mr. Hendrick, but we shall stay at Seven Hills tonight." She saw that he was about to protest and said quickly, "I assure you, we shall be very well. If you don't believe me, you are welcome to come back in the morning to see for yourself that we passed a good night."

He straightened slightly. "I just might do that, miss."

He dipped his head and left without further argument, and Marianna wondered over his obvious concern. She was a little surprised to find herself the object of anyone's sympathy for, to her way of thinking, she was the recipient of a great good fortune. She and her brother and old nurse had been living in a two-room pensioner's cottage, struggling to survive on a pitiful income, when she had written to one of her father's relatives and asked for his assistance in obtaining a suitable position. To her great surprise, she had received a prompt letter in return, from a great-uncle with whom she had never before exchanged so much as a pleasantry. A man of great kindness he must be, she reasoned, for Mr. Cecil Madison had given her not a reference or an employment, as she had so boldly asked, but an entire house of her own. A house that was, she believed, nothing short of a Godsend.

She took her first full look at the large entry hall and the rooms that opened off it. They were all wide, expansive spaces with ancient, dusty floorboards and open fireplaces. The furniture was draped in covers, and there was a pervading odor of damp and disuse. Her optimistic nature told her that she could very well dispel the mustiness of the place with some cleaning and a few fires to chase away the damp. Resolutely she ignored her more pessimistic side that warned her that keeping such rooms heated in the winter would cost a dear sum.

In the gathering darkness of evening, she made her way to the back of the house to the kitchens. Miss Blessington had cleared away the dust and dirt from one of the tables and was preparing their evening meal by the light of a single candle. She looked up with one skeptical brow raised. "Are you certain, Miss Marianna, that we are to live here—just the three of us? Why, we could never use half the rooms."

"It is a great barn of a place, isn't it?" she asked with a slight laugh. "There are a hundred things wrong with it, I fear. The furniture looks quite shabby and hopelessly out of date. There is dirt and grime everywhere, and I am certain I saw some broken windowpanes when we drove up just now. Still, it is ours, Blessing, and we can be very happy here, I think."

"I'll say no more then," Miss Blessington promised through thin lips. She turned her attention back to her work. After a moment, she said, "I'll walk into the village first thing in the morning. Heaven knows what shops I'll find; but we must have food, and I won't return until I have purchased something edible for us. Although what I am to use to buy such things, I cannot say."

"Do you think the village shops will give us credit, Blessing? After all, we are the new residents of Seven Hills. Perhaps that carries a bit of cache with the local people?"

Miss Blessington cast a caustic gaze about the dirty, outdated kitchen. "I doubt it," she said with a sniff.

"Then I shall have to think of some way to produce an income for us. I was thinking that perhaps I could give lessons—in French and Italian and perhaps some water-colors. Surely the villagers must have daughters I might be able to teach."

"Could be. But I daresay giving lessons to shopkeepers' daughters is a difficult way to earn a wage."

"I shall just have to think of something else, then," she said, refusing to allow the old woman's words to deflate her buoyant spirit. It was a resolve easier said than kept. By the time they sat down in the dimly-lit kitchen to share their evening meal, she was still unable to hit upon a scheme that might bring a regular income. She only half listened to Robin's enthusiastic descriptions of the stable accommodations.

"You must come see it first thing, Marianna, for I know you shall be astonished by the size of it. It's many times bigger than some of the houses we've seen, and a fellow can keep ever so many horses in a stable like that. Why, I should think we might allow other people to keep horses at Seven Hills, too, if we've a mind to it."

"You might as well ask for a castle in Spain," said Marianna, with a smile toward her sporting-mad brother. "I know there is nothing you would like more than to have a stable full of the finest horseflesh, but have you any notion how much it costs to keep a horse?"

"Well, no," he said, "but I should guess it costs a goodly sum, otherwise we would have a horse of our own."

"Then, Robin, dear, how could we ever hope to support and care for other people's horses?"

He cast her a look of youthful indignation. "No, no! You're not listening! I'm not suggesting we keep horses just to have them about, you know. I'm simply saying we should take in horses like boarders. You know—let people keep their horses here and have them pay us for it."

Marianna gave her head a shake. "That's a nice idea, Robin, dear, but I doubt very much that anyone would want to pay us to keep their horses for them."

"Someone might. After all, we're very near Newmarket. When the weather improves and the race courses open, I should think there will be many gentlemen who would like to see their horses kept in a stable as grand as ours."

Marianna stared at him a moment. "Do you really think so?"

"Why not? I think it's a capital notion, and just think of all the wonderful horses I could ride!"

She laughed and said no more, but found herself considering Robin's words later that night as she waited for sleep to come. She had taken one of the candles and ventured upstairs and selected a large sleeping chamber that contained an oversized bed and a daybed by the window. Like the other rooms in the house, this one smelled of stale air and musty fabric. She considered opening a window; but once the sun had gone down, the weather had turned, and a rather fierce spring wind began to howl outside. Opening a window would, she feared, only stir up all the dust and dirt in the room, and then it would be quite uninhabitable. Instead, she helped Miss Blessington carefully draw back the furniture covers so as not to shake up the dust, and they settled down for the night, with Blessing and Robin in the bed, and Marianna stretched out upon the day chaise.

In very little time she heard the sound of soft, even breathing coming from the bed and knew her brother and her old nurse were asleep. Poor darlings, how exhausted they must be, she thought. She was exhausted herself, but no matter how tired she was, sleep refused to come. Instead, she found herself thinking of Mr. Hendrick and his kind concern for their safety. She scoffed at the notion that they might be in any danger, yet as she lay upon her makeshift bed, listening to the wind whipping past the house, rattling the windows, and creaking at the old walls, her imagination began to go down dark and alarming paths.

Before long she could scarcely tell if her mind was playing tricks or if she was truly hearing uncommon noises coming from the bowels of the unfamiliar old house. She had never before been possessed of a fanciful imagination, but the wind was playing havoc with her common sense. The windows of the bedchamber opened out over the front of the house, and with every blast of wind, with every rattle of panes and shutters, her imagination ran rampant. She lay on the daybed, listening to the wind, convinced she heard the sound of horses approaching the house, of men's voices, of stealthy footsteps coming down the hall toward her room.

Her impulse was to bury her head beneath her blanket and squeeze her eyes shut until the horrid sounds went away, until daylight came again and she no longer had to fear the noises brought on by the wind and the creaking old house. But she wasn't the sort of woman who typically gave in to impulse. She was a young woman of responsibility with a family to look after and protect. And a responsible head of a family did not bury her head beneath a blanket.

Slowly, reluctantly, Marianna Madison left her bed. With her heart beating very much like the galloping horses she had imagined moments before, she crept down the stairs, determined to inspect the house and make sure it was secure.

Major Ulrick Beauleigh arrived at Seven Hills in a foul mood. It was well past midnight, he judged, and had he been a less stubborn man, he would have taken a room back at the inn that had served him his supper. He would have climbed into a soft, warm bed and put an end to the miseries of his journey. Had he been less stubborn, he wouldn't have willed himself to travel on through the dark, windy night, refusing to stop until he had arrived at last at Seven Hills.

Foolishly, he had insisted upon traveling by horseback, convinced he would make better time than he would in a traveling chaise. In the end, he had proved himself wrong. He had begun his journey early in the morning, and before the spring sun had risen high in the sky, his leg had begun to throb mercilessly, forcing him to stop with irritating regularity to walk on it, stretch it out, and regain the mastery over the old injury. To make matters worse, just past Newmarket he had developed one of those sickening headaches he had come to know all too well, a residual effect of the anesthesia the physicians had used to stitch up his leg.

Stubbornly, he fought against the headache, just as he willed away the pain that beat an agonizing tattoo along his thigh. He wasn't about to give in to such annoyances, not now, not when he was so close to home.

Home. He would spend the night in his own home or die in the attempt, and since God had proved on several previous, and more promising, occasions that He wasn't yet ready to call him home, he rather expected he would spend the night at Seven Hills. At last he would experience for himself the feeling of solitude, of knowing the place was his.

That cursed pain in his leg caused him to dismount yet again at the drive, so he had his first glimpse of Seven Hills as he led his horse up to the front door. Exhaustion tempted him to abandon his horse then and there, but he didn't. He was too disciplined and knew only too well how much a soldier had to rely upon his mount. He limped around the corner of the house, his horse following, but when he saw how far away the stable was from the manor house, his spirits sank. Behind him, the wind whipped at one of the doors to the house, sending it banging back and forth on its hinges. He tethered his horse near a patch of lawn and slowly climbed the few steps to where the door was rocking crazily. He passed through it and discovered himself in the kitchens, a vast apartment of bare floors and sturdy tables, now dingy and dusty from disuse. After securing the door, he began to rummage about, looking for a candle or a light of some kind that might allow him to catch his first glimpse of his new home.

Rooting in drawers led him to the discovery of a treasury of long-forgotten items: bits of string, tongs, poultry lacers, and a myriad of odd items he didn't recognize all jumbled together. He was pawing through them, intent upon his search for a candle, when he heard a slight noise behind him.

His reflexes, honed by years of training and months of combat, were exceptional, and he whirled about, ready to draw his weapon and bring down his attacker.

But he had no weapon, and before him stood not a soldier of Napoleon's army, but a young woman so lovely, he thought at first he was imagining things once again. She appeared to be more a vision than a reality, garbed in a loosely flowing white gown, her dark hair falling about her slim shoulders, her pale eyes enormous in her small face.

How long she had been standing there, he had no idea. What she was doing in his home, he couldn't guess. He knew only that she didn't belong there, that she was an intruder and—real or imagined—she must be made to leave.

Watching her intently, wary of any reaction, he straightened himself away from the drawer and drew himself up to his full height. Slowly, inexorably, he began to advance upon her.

Two

Astonishment rooted Marianna's feet to the floor, and she was rather incapable of any thought except that there was a stranger in her house. She could only stare at him, and he stared right back, through narrowed eyes beneath a fall of dark, rather unkempt hair. His tall body was shrouded in a long, full cape, and in the shadows of the moonlit kitchen, he looked dangerous and wholly menacing.

Suddenly shaking, she instinctively began to back her way out of the kitchen, a motion that sent his dark brows into a frown.

He took a step toward her, and her heart leapt to her throat. At last she made a sound—a high, breathy shriek—then she turned and fled the kitchen, racing down the dark corridor, almost mad with terror, on legs that felt weighted.

Her first inclination was to run upstairs, to Blessing, who had always made her feel safe before, but now it was up to Marianna to protect her old nurse and her brother, to shield them from this intruder and the danger he posed. Blindly, she threw open the first door she came to and ran to the far side of a small drawing room, to the pitiful protection of a high-backed chair.

She heard his footsteps in the corridor before she saw his silhouette appear in the doorway. He paused for what seemed very much like a lifetime before he began his slow advance into the darkened room. Slowly, deliberately, he stepped toward her.

Too late did she discover her mistake. In her panic she had run to the wrong corner of the room, away from the heavy fireplace tools that stood neatly arranged beside the old brick hearth.

With her first choice of defense very clearly out of reach, she frantically searched her corner for something—anything—she could use to defend herself against the stranger. Without thinking, she grabbed a pillow from the chair. Her body was trembling so violently, she feared she might not be able to control her movements, but she managed to hold the pillow up with the firm intention of throwing it at him.

"Don't—don't come near me," she warned in a fluttering voice.

He paused a moment and studied her, his body alert with interest. He took another slow step toward her.

Suddenly the pillow felt like a tremendous weight in her hand. It took every ounce of will she possessed to throw it at him.

It missed. The pillow whooshed neatly past his shoulder, and incredibly, Marianna heard him curse softly.

In the shadows of the room, she watched him move toward the hearth with an unnatural gait. In the next moment, he struck a light and set the nub of a candle glowing. The meager light didn't help at all; rather, it gave the room an other-worldly feeling and lent the lines and angles of his face a sharpness that made him seem more dangerous than ever.

"Who are you?" he asked, in a quiet, but firm voice, "and what are you doing in this house?"

Vaguely, Marianna realized that something in his words didn't ring true. A robber asking her name? A murderer demanding to know what she was doing in her own home?

She wanted to ask what he was talking about, but it took all her strength to keep her suddenly shaking knees from giving way beneath her. If he chose that moment to come near her, she was very well convinced that she would simply crumble into a jellied heap on the floor at his feet.

As if reading her mind, he took a step or two toward her.

"Don't come any closer!" she said on a sob. "You have no right to be in my home!"

"*Your* home?" he asked incredulously. "Good God, so that's it. I thought I was at Seven Hills, and instead I've stumbled into the wrong house!"

"But it is—! I mean, you're here—! This *is* Seven Hills."

His eyes crinkled at the corners as if he were seeing her for the first time. Resolutely, he crossed the distance between them with few steps and grasped her by the arm.

She should have fought. She should have let loose a loud and effective scream; but it suddenly seemed that he had been in her house for hours, menacing her, tormenting her, and the emotions she had been made to endure during the last few minutes became altogether too much. No longer did her mind work or her body obey her commands. Like a doll she allowed him to lead her to a chair by the fireplace. Gratefully she sat down, and he knelt down close in front of her.

"What are you doing here?" he demanded, in a much harsher voice.

She looked into his face, set in shadows by the dim light of the nearby candle. He was staring at her, his dark brows knit together in a frown and his mouth set in a hard line above the sharp angle of his jaw. He had about him a look that was unforgiving, distrustful, unmoving.

How easily he could have intimidated her! She was already at a disadvantage, for she had been frightened beyond reason just moments ago, but that was changed now. She was still a bit confused, perhaps, but she wasn't about to cower in the face of this man's rudeness. Her chin went up a bit.

"I live here," she said, with as much dignity as a lady clad in only a nightdress could muster.

"Oh, no, you don't, my dear young woman. If this is Seven Hills, as you say, then you are trespassing. This is my property."

She gave her head a slight shake as if by doing so she could clear it of all the confusion and bewilderment she was feeling. "Your property? But *I* am the owner of Seven Hills! My great-uncle Madison made me a gift of it."

Two lines of concentration appeared above the bridge of his straight nose. "Madison?"

"That's right," she answered. "I am Miss Madison and this is my house and I—I want you to leave." She had intended to sound authoritative, even regal; but her voice had caught on a sob, and she rather suspected she had sounded more childish than commanding.

"Madison," he said again, and this time one of his dark brows flew skeptically. "That's a name I recognize."

She couldn't help but feel a swell of relief. Apparently, her family name did carry some weight with the local people after all. "Then, you'll leave immediately?"

"Leave? Oh, far from it, I assure you," he replied, standing and staring down at her with a hard glare. "This estate is mine. I bought it, I own it, and no one makes a charlie of Rick Beauleigh."

"A charlie?" she repeated, frowning slightly. "You make it sound as if I've cheated you somehow. Indeed, how could I when I have never met you before in my life!"

"One need not claim an acquaintance to lead a man like a tame fool on a string. I'm beginning to see your game quite clearly now."

"There is no game here, sir!" she protested indignantly.

"Isn't there? I've heard of schemes such as this. First you entice an unsuspecting pigeon to buy your property; then—once you have his money—you switch the castle for the merest shack or simply deny that there was ever any bargain struck at all. I assure you, I won't be lead such a dance."

She drew a deep breath and stood, planting a hand on each hip in what she hoped was a position of calm authority. "Nor will I allow you to speak to me in such a manner, sir, and I must insist . . ." Her remaining words died away at the sight of his changing expression.

His dark brows rose in fascination as his gaze swept over the thin material of her nightdress and the outline of her slim figure silhouetted against the light of the candle. A hot flush of color covered her cheeks, and for a moment, she stood rooted to the spot, mortified, and a little bit shocked by the look he had given her. After a moment, he swung his heavy cape from his back and drew it about her shoulders, enveloping her completely, its length puddling on the floor about her feet.

Far from appreciative of his gesture, Marianna glared at him. "Insulting swine! I should think I would be safe in my own home from the unwanted attentions of a—a goose-quill gentleman! I insist you leave at once."

His brows came together in anger, but he said, in a calm tone, "I'm not leaving."

Marianna felt the color drain from her face. "But you can't stay," she said weakly. "You can't possibly stay here!"

"I can, and I will. If my spending the night here offends your sensibilities, I suggest you find other accommodations."

Clearly, they were at an impasse, she realized, for he refused to leave, and she couldn't possibly leave—not now—not in the middle of the night with a boy and an elderly woman in tow with nowhere to go. A myriad of emotions swept through her—frustration, anger, and an unfortunate urge to cry—and all the while the man merely stood regarding her with the calm detachment of one who had no regard for the damage he was causing with his simple presence. All she could think to do was escape, and without another word, she swept past him and made for the door.

She stopped at the threshold and turned to face him, determined to somehow gain the upper hand and show this insufferable man that she was a force to be reckoned with. "I expect you to be gone before morning, sir. I shall not be seeing you again."

She half walked, half ran up the stairs to her room, and for the first time in her life, she wished she had a lock on her chamber door. The home she had been promised as her own, which held such hopes for refurbishing with loving care, seemed no longer the haven she thought it would be. She half expected that horrid man to come barging through the bedroom door at any minute, insolently staring at her every curve beneath her nightdress. A flare of embarrassment flooded her cheeks.

But when she thought about the things he had said to her and the smug, calm manner in which he had stalked her in her own home, her embarrassment turned to anger. Hateful man! Did he truly think he could bully her out of her own home? Did he actually think he had merely to arrive in the middle of the night and claim Seven Hills as his own and expect her to simply leave, no questions asked?

She flung his cape from her shoulders as if it were on fire and settled down upon the daybed, knowing she was too angry to sleep. She was angry that a brazen stranger could arrogantly assume he could wrest her home from her, but she was also angry with herself, for having allowed him and his insufferable manners to turn her into a scared rabbit. She wouldn't allow it to happen again. She had a family to provide for, and she wasn't about to give up Seven Hills without a fight. She would think of a way to get him out of her house if she had to stay up all night to do it.

Three

Marianna didn't stay up all night. Rather, she was asleep within minutes, and when she awoke the spring sun was streaming through the windows. Robin and Miss Blessington were nowhere in sight, and the bed on which they had slept was neatly made up.

She jumped off the daybed and made hasty work of her morning ablutions, all the while berating herself for having slept so long. Poor Robin and Blessing were alone downstairs with that horrid man, with no one to protect them. *If he upsets Miss Blessington or Robin* . . . she thought furiously.

She flew down the stairs and made her way to the kitchens. From the other side of the door she heard the chinking sound of pottery being handled and of footfalls on the old hardwood floor. Anger rose in her like a swelling wave. She flung the door open and marched in, prepared to do battle.

Miss Blessington was there, quite alone, and engaged in cleaning the kitchen from top to bottom. The room was warm and full of sunlight and the aroma of toasted bread. She was on the far side of the room, her arms sunk elbow-deep in a huge basin of water, as she prepared to mop the last of the cupboards still covered with dust. She looked up briefly and said, "There you are. I was beginning to think you might sleep the day away."

A tide of relief washed over her. She and Miss Blessington were alone, and there was no sign of last night's intruder. Perhaps he had come to his senses after all and left Seven Hills. She said placidly, "You should have wakened me, Blessing. How long have you and Robin been up?"

"Since daylight," said the old woman, as she slapped a soaking wet rag onto a cupboard and began to scrub furiously. "Master Robin was anxious to be down again at the stables. Imagine his delight to find that there was actually a horse there this morning."

Marianna frowned. "Then, he's still here!"

"He?" repeated Miss Blessington. "Is he a caretaker, then? A man engaged to look after the property?"

"No, not exactly," said Marianna slowly, as she tried to think of a way to break the news that an interloper was laying claim to their home.

Miss Blessington abandoned her work and fixed Marianna with a pointed look. "And what, pray, do you mean by that?"

She had never been able to withstand her old nurse's penetrating gaze and felt at once as if she were back in the schoolroom, enduring a scold over some thoughtless bit of mischief. Marianna found herself looking for ways to downplay the incidents of the night before, and said, "He is simply a man—a gentleman, I believe—who is possibly just a bit confused."

"That he must be, as well as you. I won't ask what he's doing here, Miss Marianna, for I think you know already you cannot have a man in this house—"

"Blessing, I know, truly I do!" she exclaimed. "I tried to make him leave last night, but he insists he owns Seven Hills. He said he bought it and he won't be made to give it up."

"He must be made to."

"I know, I know," said Marianna, and her shoulders sagged slightly at the mere prospect of having to go another round of argument with the man. "I shall try to reason with him once more."

"And if he doesn't agree to go willingly?" asked Miss Blessington, with typical pessimism.

"Then I-I shall petition my great-uncle Madison for help," she replied, seizing upon the only remedy she could think of. "Uncle Madison will prove once and for all that I am the owner of Seven Hills, and not that horrid man."

"And if your uncle won't help?"

"I don't know, but I daresay I shall think of something. Perhaps I shall not need my uncle's assistance after all. Perhaps I shall be able to convince the man to leave willingly."

Even as she said those words, she didn't believe them. She had little trouble recalling the look of determination on his face as he argued with her last night, and when she chanced to recall, with stunning clarity, the insolent manner in which his eyes had raked over every curve of her body beneath her nightdress, a flare of angry embarrassment warmed her.

Marianna didn't have to search long before finding the major in a first-floor room that was full, from floor to ceiling, with books. He was casually lounging against a corner of the bookshelves, quite at his ease, and thumbing through the pages of a rather slim volume. At her entrance, he looked up, but he didn't alter his posture. Rather, it seemed to Marianna that he appeared as relaxed as if he were in his own home, in his own library, perusing familiar books that had been handed down from one generation of his family to the next.

But he wasn't in his own home—he was in *her* home. *She* owned Seven Hills, and she wasn't about to allow him to snatch it from beneath her. Resolutely, she squared her shoulders and walked up to face him.

Thankfully, he didn't appear quite so menacing in the light of day, although he was still somehow a bit intimidating. It was all she could do to ignore the way her heart began to skip as she stood in front of him, and she had to make a conscious effort to remind herself that she couldn't afford to anger him as she had the night before.

As on the occasion of their first meeting, his appearance was just a bit unkempt. Above his aristocratic cheekbones, tiny lines fanned out from the corners of his blue eyes. His dark hair was a little too long, his skin a bit too tanned, and he wore his well-tailored clothes with a casual ease that was oddly elegant.

But what caught her attention and held it was his face. He had about him the expression of one who had seen a lot of the world and had spent his time lifting a rather cynical eyebrow at everything luckless enough to fall beneath his notice. Even now he was watching her through unwavering blue eyes alight with interest, as if he half expected her to suddenly stand upon her ear.

"Good morning, sir," she said, with a composure that surprised her. "I see you have not changed your mind during the night."

"Not at all, I assure you," he replied, with the slightest of bows. "Nor, I imagine, have you, else we wouldn't be having this conversation. Suppose you sit down and we'll discuss our situation calmly."

Mulishly, her chin went up as she watched him take a seat behind the massive oak desk. She had entered the room with every intention of proving to this arrogant man that he had no authority here, that he had no rights or privileges when it came to Seven Hills, yet there he sat, completely at his ease, ordering her to sit down. Such crust!

One look at his face told her that he had gauged her thoughts exactly. He was regarding her with that same look of intense interest that made her react by pressing her lips into a thin, defiant line as she slid onto one of the chairs by the desk.

"Very well," he said, smiling faintly. "Why don't you tell me your name?"

She returned his look with what she hoped was cool disdain. "I told you my name last night," she said stiffly.

His brow shot up. "And I told you my name last night, as well, but I doubt you recall it." Her sudden look of surprise convinced him he was right. "Just so. Now, perhaps you'd like to tell me your name."

"Marianna Madison," she said, wishing she knew how it was he had the power to make her behave so foolishly.

"And my name is Beauleigh," he said, with a short nod. "Ulrick Beauleigh." He watched her absorb this information. "Does the name mean anything to you?"

"Certainly not. Should it?"

"Not at all," he answered mildly. "Now, suppose we discuss our predicament."

"There's no predicament, sir. You are an intruder in my home. My uncle Madison gave me Seven Hills. If you contact him, he'll confirm it for you."

"Oh, I shall be contacting Mr. Madison," he said grimly, "but not to confirm anything."

"What do you mean?"

"Isn't it obvious? Your uncle is trying to swindle me out of the money I gave him to buy this place. You might be in on the plot, too, for all I know—"

"I would never, never do such a thing!" she protested, in high offense.

"That remains to be seen. In the meantime, I'll visit

Mr. Madison. I'll also visit the solicitor who handled all
the details of the sale. I intend to see that your uncle—and
anyone else involved in this little scheme to cheat me—is
punished. Have I made myself clear, Miss Madison?"

"You needn't make such accusations, I assure you."

"I think I'm justified until someone proves me wrong.
And I think I should warn you that my solicitor is a very
learned gentleman who is well respected in Newmarket
and in London. He'll do whatever it takes to ensure I am
declared the owner of Seven Hills."

She sat staring at him. Only yesterday her life had been
happy. She had been looking forward, secure that her
troubles were behind her and that life at last was looking
a bit rosier. Now she was faced with disaster again—disaster brought by a man who could no doubt well afford
a score of solicitors who could cunningly convince a
court that Seven Hills didn't belong to her.

"There's no need to look as if you're about to be swal-
lowed up," he said abruptly.

"But I—if we don't have Seven Hills, where will we
go?"

"We?" he repeated, his brows knit into a frown.

"My younger brother and his nurse and me."

"That isn't my affair. Surely you have only to apply to
a relative for assistance."

"There is no one but my uncle that I know of, and he
said he couldn't help us except to give me Seven Hills.
He—he doesn't wish us to live with him."

He stared at her a minute, then asked incredulously,
"Are you telling me that there's no one else? That *you're*
the head of your family?"

She heard the accusation in his tone, and a sense of
panic began to take hold of her. "It isn't as if I haven't
tried, but when my father died, he was heavily in debt
and everything was sold—the house, everything! There

was no one to turn to, except a neighbor who let us have a tenant cottage—!" She stopped short, realizing she had been babbling, revealing too much, showing him a weaker side to her nature that he would undoubtedly use to his own advantage.

He was silent for a moment, then looked away from her and ran a hand slowly through his lush hair. "Oh, God," he said wearily.

Marianna watched as he stood up and moved with a slight hitch to his step over to the long windows that lined one side of the room. He didn't seem angry anymore, but he certainly wasn't pleased; and she wondered what words she could say that would convince him she was telling the truth and that he must abandon his plan to live at Seven Hills.

There was silence. Then he turned and asked abruptly, "Isn't this home a little large for a young woman alone in the world?"

"I'm not alone," she said, sounding a trifle resentful. "I have my family with me."

"A boy and an old woman? They can't be much help to you. How old is the boy?"

"He's ten, but he's very mature for his age," she said weakly, and instantly berated herself for having said something so foolish.

"I imagine he is. He's no doubt also a bit sporting-mad, as most boys his age are."

"It's his dream to own a horse of his own, but that shall have to wait, I'm afraid."

"He'll wait forever if you live here. Horses aren't bought with buttermilk and a smile, Miss Madison. They cost dearly, as does this house. I don't see how you can provide your brother with both, based on your rather straitened circumstances."

"I know that," she said defensively. "But it's more important that we have a roof over our heads. Robin knows he must make sacrifices, too."

"And how do you intend to live? If you're facing the wind as you say you are, you won't be able to afford to light the fires in this place, to say nothing of maintaining it on a daily basis. How will you live?"

He was looking skeptically at her, and she cast her mind wildly about for inspiration. "I-I thought I would take in boarders," she heard herself say, as Robin's words from the night before leapt to mind. "We're situated very close to Newmarket, and once the courses open and racing season starts, there will be scores of people who will prefer to pass their stay in a genteel country home rather than a noisy Newmarket inn."

"You won't convince a cat to pay you to stay in one of these rooms. This house is in no condition to accept boarders."

"Not now, perhaps, but the rooms are only in want of a cleaning and a few repairs."

"And how will you pay for those repairs?"

"I-I shall give lessons to children in the village—Italian and French and watercolors," she said rashly.

He was silent again, his blue eyes watching her intently for so long she had to fight back the impulse to squirm under his gaze. Instead, she rose to her feet and said accusingly, "You don't think I can do it, do you?"

"On the contrary, I was thinking you don't appear to be meant for that kind of work."

"I daresay I might enjoy it," she said, but her words sounded unconvincing, even to her own ears. In truth, she didn't think she would enjoy giving lessons at all, just as she didn't enjoy being the only breadwinner or making family decisions that would best be left to someone possessed of wisdom and sense beyond her nineteen years.

There were too many times when the responsibility of it all seemed almost too much to bear.

She looked up at him, her gray eyes searching for some sign that he might be softening a bit. Instead, she found his expression dark and distant, his blue eyes harsh and distrustful. She knew in that instant that he would take Seven Hills away, with no more than a mere whimper of conscience.

Desperate, she abandoned all claims to pride, and asked, "Please, won't you leave? I am certain my uncle Madison will give you your money back."

"Seven Hills is mine. I'm not leaving."

"Please," she said again, taking a short, tentative step in his direction. "I appeal to you as a gentleman."

"A goose-quill gentleman?" he asked, one of his dark brows flying. "You'd be wasting your breath, I'm afraid, Marianna."

She stiffened, not at all certain she liked hearing her name on his lips. Half of her wanted to berate him for taking such liberty, while her practical side wanted to appease him, reason with him, and do whatever was necessary to convince him that he was wrong, that Seven Hills belonged to her.

She was uncertain of his power, unsure if he truly did have the wherewithal to force her from her home. She felt torn: she wanted to hate him, yet she thought it best to placate him, as well. She raised her chin slightly. "Have you had your breakfast yet?"

His blue eyes lit with interest. "I must say, you're the most well-mannered adversary I've ever come up against."

"Simply because we are at brass rags with each other doesn't mean we cannot be civil," she said coldly.

A hint of amusement played with the corners of his mouth. "True enough, Miss Madison."

"If you'll come with me, Blessing will have a meal prepared, I'm certain."

She led the way to the kitchens, supremely conscious of his presence behind her as he followed her through the corridors of the house.

Thanks to Miss Blessington's efforts, the newly cleaned kitchen was rather inviting. A fire was burning brightly and combined with the aroma of fresh bread to present a very cozy atmosphere. Miss Blessington was not alone. Mr. Hendrick was seated at the heavy oak table, patiently waiting as Miss Blessington poured out a cup of tea for him. When Marianna entered with Mr. Beauleigh, they both looked up, Miss Blessington with a look of patent disapproval upon her face, Mr. Hendrick with an expression of frowning concern.

Marianna provided a rather curt introduction all around, adding, "Blessing, he is the gentleman we were speaking of earlier."

Rick cocked a questioning brow. "Blessing? An unusual name."

"It's Blessington, actually, sir," muttered the old woman.

He said politely, "Then, you must be Miss Madison's nurse. She speaks of you in glowing terms." Mr. Beauleigh accompanied this comment by extending his hand, a gesture which took a good deal of the scowl from Miss Blessington's face. He turned and flicked a quizzical look upon Mr. Hendrick, saying, "How do you do? Are you an employee here?"

Upon first sight of Rick Beauleigh, Mr. Hendrick was prepared to distrust him. He didn't, as a rule, appreciate strangers, and since this one resembled a good number of society's gentlemen who descended upon Newmarket every year with pockets of money and a penchant toward scandalous behavior, he was quite ready to dislike him.

But no sooner did Rick hold out his hand, than the cart driver found himself a bit disconcerted. "No, sir—I mean, I don't work here, sir, although my father did years ago. I live in the village, sir, and come this morning to see to the miss's welfare, is all."

Miss Blessington set the pot of tea upon the table and cast a meaningful look at Rick. "You'll be sharing our breakfast," she said, as if the thought that he might decline such an invitation never occurred to her. " 'Tisn't much, but it will have to do until I get some food in. Miss Marianna, if I cannot buy on the nod, I shall need the last of your money, I'm afraid."

Marianna nodded, deeply aware that Mr. Beauleigh had heard Blessing's ill-chosen words. He now knew very well, if he ever had any doubt, that she had no money with which to repair Seven Hills and no money with which to pay solicitors to fight to keep her home, while he appeared to have all the money in the world. He was standing at the heavy oak table in the center of the room with infuriating ease, waiting to be fed his breakfast. By contrast, Marianna's mind was spinning, searching for some way to ensure she would keep Seven Hills and see the last of Ulrick Beauleigh.

"You sit down, Miss Marianna, and eat your breakfast while it's warm," said Miss Blessington.

"I'm not hungry," she answered, "and I've a score of things to do. You'll forgive me, please, if I don't join you, Mr. Beauleigh."

He looked at her with an expression of dark surprise. "Miss Madison, I didn't mean to intrude. If there isn't enough food for—"

"Not at all, I assure you! I simply have no appetite this morning." She turned to the cart driver, saying, "Mr. Hendrick, will you be good enough to drive me into the village? I can be ready in only minutes if you are willing."

Mr. Hendrick shuffled to his feet. "I shall drive ye, sure, miss, but shouldn't ye have a tea first?"

"Not at all, although I hope you will have a cup while I get ready. I won't be long," she promised. With her next breath she was out the door and hurrying toward her room, where she donned bonnet, gloves and pelisse. All the while, she entertained the happy thought that she was about to gain an advantage over Mr. Beauleigh. While he was enjoying the breakfast Blessing had prepared, she would be appealing to her uncle Madison. With any luck, she would secure Uncle Madison's assistance in evicting Mr. Beauleigh from Seven Hills before he took his last bite of breakfast.

Four

As Marianna rode along in the little cart, she cast a glance at Mr. Hendrick, and said, "Tell me, do you know my uncle Madison? What sort of man is he?"

"Now, which Mr. Madison would that be, miss?"

"Why, Mr. Cecil Madison, of course!" she replied, with some surprise.

"Ah, miss, I don't know much about 'im, but he do have a large house, and he do keep to 'isself."

"He must be a very kind man, the sort of man to whom the neighbors turn in times of trouble?"

Mr. Hendrick ran a hand across his stubbled chin. "Now, miss, I wouldn't think so," he said after a bit of thought.

"Well, what sort of man is he? Can you describe him to me?"

"No, miss, I don't think I ought. Ain't my place, if ye know what I mean, and besides, I don't see much of the gentleman. Nobody does. He don't go out much among the neighborhood, if you understand my meaning, but keeps to 'isself in a big house many times the size of Seven Hills."

"Perhaps he's lonely," Marianna said thoughtfully. "Perhaps he shall be glad of my company and won't think ill of me for calling upon him unannounced."

She was still hoping that to be the case a little while

later as Mr. Hendrick drew the old cart to a stop before the front door of a large home that stood isolated just outside the village. It was an imposing building, with a large portico and a stately front door. Marianna grasped the knocker and gave it a light rap and was a little surprised when the door opened almost instantly.

A liveried footman looked down upon her, and nodded slightly when she inquired if Mr. Madison was at home.

"Please tell him his niece—his great-niece—Miss Marianna Madison is calling on a matter of importance—great importance!—if you would be so kind."

The footman bowed and ushered her into the house, then led her across the vast hall to a small drawing room. She swept past him into the room and heard the door close softly behind her. She was grateful to find herself alone, for from the moment she had set the knocker to rapping, she had begun to entertain second thoughts about her visit. She was far from certain that her uncle Madison would welcome her or lend assistance, for in his one, brief letter to her, he had stated in no uncertain terms that his gift of Seven Hills represented all the patronage she could expect from him.

Now, as she waited in the small room for what seemed to be an inordinately long period of time, she wondered if he would be angry with her or if perhaps he might refuse to see her altogether. Then what would she do?

She was saved the trouble of allowing her imagination to scamper farther down such desperate paths when the door opened again. She sprang to her feet, nervous, uncertain, and ready to beg her uncle's forgiveness for the intrusion.

But it was not her uncle who entered the room. A striking young woman of perhaps twenty-two summers swept regally across the threshold. She was dressed in the height of fashion, and her brown hair was possessed of fiery red lights that shimmered among the curls scattered atop her head. Her green eyes regarded Marianna with cool measure. In short, she was quite stunning, rather exotic, and wholly unlike any woman Marianna had ever seen before.

"I understand you wish to speak to my uncle," said the woman in a tone laden with mistrust. "I am his niece, Isabelle Madison."

"Then, we are cousins!" exclaimed Marianna, as she dipped a short curtsy. "Tell me, do you live here? Can you describe to me what kind of a man my great-uncle is?"

"He's the kind who doesn't care to be bothered by importunate relatives, if that answers your question," said Miss Madison, as she looked Marianna up and down.

Marianna was far from offended by the gesture, for she knew she wasn't looking her best. Her straw bonnet was plain and unadorned; her dress had been new two years before and was slightly out of fashion and certainly well-worn. The fabric of her pelisse had begun to shine at the elbows from use, and her shoes had not been polished in a week. She hardly presented the picture of a young lady of breeding, so it was little wonder that Isabelle Madison should regard her with such skepticism.

"I assure you, I haven't come to plague Great-uncle Madison with requests," she said mildly.

Isabelle appeared unconvinced. "Indeed? Then, perhaps you will be good enough to tell me your business with him?"

"I have come about Seven Hills—do you know it?"

Isabelle sank with studied grace upon a nearby chair. "Of course."

"Then, you must know, too, that Uncle Madison gave it to me—to me and my family. We have no one, you see, and nowhere to go and—"

"Yes, I know of your circumstance and I know Uncle

Madison gave you Seven Hills. Isn't it enough? Must you have more?" she asked pettishly.

"Oh, no, ma'am, you misunderstand me! I am not here to ask Uncle Madison for anything else! How could I, when he has been generosity itself! I simply wish to thank him and to ask—if, indeed, it isn't too much trouble—for his assistance in the merest of troubles. You see, there is a man—he's there right now, in fact—who insists that *he* owns Seven Hills. He will not believe me when I tell him the place belongs to me. I-I was hoping my uncle would help—that he would tell this-this *usurper* that he has no claim to Seven Hills and he must leave at once."

"Isn't it enough my uncle made you a gift of the place?" Isabelle asked, with some annoyance. "Must he police it for you, too?"

"I don't mean to make my problem his," said Marianna, with a quick step forward, "but I thought if my uncle spoke to the man, if he told Mr. Beauleigh he must leave at once and abandon his ridiculous claim—"

"Beauleigh?" repeated Isabelle, her attention arrested. "Did you just say the man's name is Beauleigh?"

"Why, yes, although I cannot see what difference—"

"Describe him," commanded Isabelle imperiously.

Marianna cast her mind's eye back to that morning. "Well, let me think. He's rather tall with dark hair and blue eyes. He—he has a bit of an injury of some sort to one leg, and he has a rather insistent way about him." She watched for Miss Madison's reaction to this rather vague description and was somewhat surprised to see a woman of such polish spring to her feet and begin to pace furtively about the room.

After a moment Isabelle stopped and cast Marianna a penetrating look. "I shall not promise to help you, but I shall see the situation for myself."

"Oh—oh, thank you!" Marianna exclaimed, with undisguised relief. "But I shouldn't wish to disturb you, for it truly isn't your affair. Perhaps if I could simply speak to my uncle—"

"Cecil Madison is not taking callers, and even if he were, he isn't likely to be disposed to help you. Oh, don't look so stricken, for he isn't the sort of man to help anyone, but I may be able to convince him otherwise in your case."

"I shall be ever so grateful to you."

"We shall see. Only tell me, are you certain of this man's name?" she asked, casting Marianna a rather unnerving gaze.

"I can only tell you what was said to me, and he did tell me his name was Beauleigh. Mr. Ulrick Beauleigh."

"Very well. You may go now. I shall speak to my uncle and shall come to you presently at Seven Hills."

"Oh, dear, *dear* cousin! How good you are!"

Isabelle held up one soft, white hand. "Please don't rely too much upon me, for I shall not have your disappointment on my hands. I promise nothing, you know," she said, as she led the way to the door.

But Marianna was hopeful for the first time since having made the acquaintance of the insufferable Mr. Beauleigh. Life, she believed, was beginning to look a bit rosier, and before the day was through, her encounter with Mr. Beauleigh would be nothing but a distasteful memory, Seven Hills would be hers, and she and her little family would be quite happy. It only remained for Mr. Beauleigh to be brought to his senses and made to leave.

Mr. Ulrick Beauleigh was thinking very much the same thing about Marianna Madison as he stared incredulously at his longtime friend and solicitor, John Bagwell. "Can she not be made to leave?" he demanded.

"By rights, you shouldn't be there either, Rick," said Mr. Bagwell calmly. "No one should have possession of Seven Hills until the question of its ownership is resolved. Frankly, I'm a little astonished that there really is a great-niece. I had thought she would turn out to be nothing more than a product of old Mr. Cecil's imagination."

"She's real, I assure you," said Rick dryly, "as is her intrusion in my life."

"She's no doubt thinking the very same thing of you," said Mr. Bagwell, with a slight smile. "We could solve this whole business easily enough, you know."

Rick looked at him, his blue eyes alight with interest. "How?"

"I'll speak to Mr. Arthur and convince him to give you your money back. That way, Miss Madison will have the property and you'll be free to purchase another estate equally to your liking."

"But there is no other estate equally to my liking," said Rick evenly.

"Are you telling me that only Seven Hills will do?"

He nodded briefly. "Only Seven Hills."

"Can you tell me why?"

Rick looked at him, his expression bland. "No."

Mr. Bagwell sighed. "As your solicitor I should ask why you insist upon making your life so needlessly difficult. As your friend, I shall let the question pass."

It was a wise thing to do, reflected Rick, for he had no intention of telling his friend the reason he must own Seven Hills and no other. He said, instead, with a violence of feeling, "This entire business is nonsense, you know. Good God, man, you handled the sale yourself! *I* own Seven Hills."

"And so I believe, but we must be certain. As I said before, Mr. Cecil's papers appear to be in order. It will simply take some time to verify whether or not they are, after all, authentic."

"And in the meantime, what am I to do?"

"The first thing you must do is remove yourself from the premises. You cannot continue to remain in the house with a young, unmarried woman."

"Oh, yes, I can," said Rick grimly.

Mr. Bagwell frowned. "That's not very sporting of you. Only think of the girl's reputation."

"I prefer to think of my home and what she'll do to it if left to her own devices. Did I tell you, she insists upon turning the place into a hotel? If I leave, there will be no one to stop her preposterous plan."

"I'll speak to her," said Mr. Bagwell with the calm assurance of a man used to wielding his authority.

"I hope you may make her see reason. God knows she won't listen to me."

"Is she a very calculating young woman, would you say?"

Rick looked up quickly. "Not at all. She's little more than a child, really, and I don't think her back is broad enough to bear as much as she thinks."

"Perhaps her circumstances are not so very thin."

"If only half of what she has said is true, they are. She has no income, yet she has assumed the responsibility of supporting and caring for a tad of a brother and an old nurse who must be more hindrance than help to her."

"Where are her parents?"

"She mentioned her father had died, and I can only assume her mother is gone, too." He had a sudden thought and asked, "What about these uncles—the ones that are fighting over the property? Perhaps one of them could be persuaded to take her—"

Mr. Bagwell cut him off, saying, "Arthur Madison would sooner take a bite out of his own arm than share a crumb with someone in need. His brother Cecil is, I'm afraid, of no more generous disposition."

"But he gave the house to her, didn't he?"

"Only to best his brother. He could have bequeathed it with equal relish to a cat, but he probably couldn't find one at the time. Truly, Rick, the Madison brothers come from a miserly family and have always carried their charity in their breeches' pockets. They won't help her."

"It's a pity," said Rick Beauleigh thoughtfully. "When all this is over and she is made to leave Seven Hills, I wonder what shall become of her?"

That thought was still with him a little later as he left John Bagwell's Newmarket office to ride back to Seven Hills. He swung himself slowly up into the saddle and set off at an even pace, hoping he would make it back before his bad leg began to trouble him. He didn't, of course, and before very long his leg began to throb. He was about to stop and walk on it when he spotted Marianna ahead of him, slowly walking down the road that circled the boundary of Seven Hills.

He spurred his horse on and drew alongside her, saying, "Good morning, Miss Madison."

Startled, she looked up in time to see him touch his gloved hand to the brim of his hat. He looked quite imposing astride his horse, a magnificent black creature of perhaps fifteen hands, with sleek, well-muscled shoulders and a long, intelligent head. It was the kind of horse that would send her brother mad with delight, and she hoped the animal and its owner were gone before Robin got a chance to become too attached to it.

She said civilly, "Good morning. Have you been to the village?"

"To Newmarket, actually. I had business there. May I walk with you the rest of the way?" He swung slowly down from the saddle and gathered the reins in his hands.

Her first reaction was to answer him curtly, to fend off his attempts at courtesy in retaliation for his previous behavior. But then Marianna chanced to recall her encounter with Isabelle Madison, and a vision took form in her mind's eye of her Madison cousin, descending upon Seven Hills in her defense, driving evil Rick Beauleigh from her home. In a matter of a few short hours, she believed, he would be made to abandon his claim to the place, leaving her the sole and rightful owner.

In the face of such a happy fantasy, she saw no reason she should not be civil to the poor man. "I had business this morning, too," she said with a satisfied smile.

He fell into step beside her, and from beneath the brim of her bonnet, she cast a quick glance at his legs, curious over the injury that caused his slight limp, wondering if he wouldn't be more comfortable riding, rather than walking. She noted that his complexion was rather pale, and there was a tightness to his lips as he strode beside her.

She was certain he would not allow the merest sympathy, but said, anyway, "You mustn't let me keep you, sir, if you would prefer to ride."

In actual fact, his leg had begun to feel better the moment he had got down from his horse, and the few steps he had taken had already begun to work a kind of therapy upon his old injury. He said genially, "Not at all. I shall enjoy the walk. As a matter of fact, I was about to suggest that we leave the road at this point and travel across that field there. The walk is an enjoyable one, and the approach to Seven Hills is much more scenic."

Marianna hesitated, but since she could not think of a single reason why she should not comply with such a polite invitation, she left the road and began to walk across the rolling fields.

They walked for some time in silence before Rick said,

"I should tell you, I think, that I visited my solicitor this morning."

If he thought to make her quake with that revelation, he was mistaken. Marianna looked up at him quite unafraid and countered, "And I visited my uncle Madison."

"Mr. Cecil Madison, is it? The uncle who bequeathed you Seven Hills?"

"Why, yes! How did you know?"

"Because I have had the entire story from John Bagwell. He is the solicitor who represented me in my purchase of the property. He is also the solicitor for Mr. Cecil Madison and his brother, Arthur."

"Then, your solicitor—your Mr. Bagwell—is very well acquainted with the true owner of Seven Hills. I hope he was kind to you when he told you that you must leave the place," she said generously.

His eyes sparked with what she considered a rather ill-judged humor. "On the contrary, ma'am. It seems the question of ownership is very much unresolved."

Her steps came to a sudden halt, and she stared up at him. "How can that be?"

"It seems both Madison brothers believe they are the owner of the property and each planned to dispose of it without consulting the other."

"Are you saying that one brother sold it to you while the other brother gave it to me?" she demanded.

"So it appears, but you needn't tease yourself over it. John Bagwell will have the matter sorted out, and he'll propose a fair resolution. You may trust him, you know."

"Trust him? Trust *your* solicitor? The very solicitor you said could convince a court of anything you desired? No, I thank you!" she retorted, setting off again at a much brisker pace.

Rick matched her stride for stride. "John Bagwell may be in my employ, but he is a man of honor, Miss Madison.

He will not be compelled to behave in a less than gentlemanly fashion."

"How can I be certain of that?" she demanded. "I don't even know the man."

"But I do. I've known him since our days together at school. He comes from a good family, his motives are pure and he's possessed of the highest ideals. When I was out of the country for a time, he managed my affairs well. I would trust no other to do so."

Marianna considered these words even while she insisted to herself that Rick Beauleigh's opinion meant nothing to her.

"I'm afraid I cannot wait until your Mr. Bagwell comes to a decision," she said. "Our situation must be resolved now."

"Why so?"

"Because I cannot wait to settle into the place, to begin making the changes that need to be made."

"Do you still intend to turn Seven Hills into an inn?"

"As soon as possible. Without an income from paying guests, my family cannot live."

"I won't allow you to do so, Marianna." He spoke the words quietly, yet there was a power beneath them, an underlying resolution that set her immediately on her guard.

Her steps halted, and she faced him defiantly. "I will not meekly relinquish my home—the home that was given to me—that belongs to me!"

"Nor will I," he said, quite simply. "So it seems we are once again at dagger drawing."

"I shall not back down," she warned. "I shall stay at Seven Hills until I am carried out!"

"A delightful prospect, and one to which I shall look forward," he said with infuriating calm. "But tell me—if you refuse to leave and I decline to do the same, does that mean we shall be sharing the place?"

For a moment words failed her. "But I thought—I thought you were merely trying to frighten me—to convince me to desert my claim. Do you mean you truly will not go? You honestly refuse to leave?"

"With all my heart," he said, with another hint of that annoying smile.

She set off again, saying furiously, "Let me assure you, sir, that I am not going anywhere. My family and I are staying! Uncle Madison will see to that!"

"Then, you must be prepared to bear the consequences."

She cast him an incredulous look. "Are you threatening me?"

"No, but I am educating you a bit in the ways of the world. What do you think the neighborhood shall think when they discover you and I are sharing a house—even a large house, such as Seven Hills?"

"I—I hadn't thought of it," she said, in some confusion as her steps slowed. "What is it anyone's business? What could they possibly have to say?"

"Plenty, I should think," he said evenly, "and it won't be my reputation that shall be made to suffer. They'll label you, Marianna. They'll think you a scarlet woman for living in the same house with a man who is not your husband or a relation of any kind."

Speechless, she stared up at him. "They—they wouldn't!"

"Don't be naive," he recommended. And yet, he couldn't help but observe that she was very naive, indeed. She was looking up at him, her bonnet framing her face as if it were a fine painting. For the first time, Rick was struck by how pretty she was. Her black curls were shining in the sunlight, and her gray eyes searched his as a parade of emotions crossed her expressive face.

In that moment she realized what kind of adversary he was: the kind of foe who would marshal whatever means necessary to win. There was something ruthless about him, something wholly merciless that told her he would not be dissuaded. Almost did she relent; indeed, it seemed he had every advantage in the situation, while she had none. It was truly tempting to just abandon the fight, to let him have the place, to slip away quietly into the night without having to endure any more of his unpleasantness.

But where would she go? And what would become of Robin and Blessing? They had nothing to live on and no prospects for a roof over their heads. She had no choice but to fight, to remain where she was.

Marianna squared her shoulders, ready to do battle. "I won't give up. I won't leave Seven Hills willingly."

"Valiantly put, but don't suppose that simply because you occupy a room there, you may have your way with the place. Until our dispute is resolved, there shall be no tenants at Seven Hills," he said purposefully.

"But how are we to live?"

"I cannot advise you," he said, unmoved. "You shall have to devise your own scheme."

"Of all the callous, unfeeling—!" She stopped, almost choking on emotion. "Very well, Mr. Beauleigh! We are now past rattling our sabers at each other, I think."

"As you say, madam," he answered, with a slight bow.

"Tell me once and at last: will you or will you not leave Seven Hills?"

"I will not," said Rick, very evenly.

"Very well! If you will not leave, you may—you may sleep in the barn!"

"I assure you, I shall sleep wherever I like. And I'm not averse to sharing a bed, if the mood strikes me."

It was a mean thing to say, a statement not at all worthy of a gentleman of his rank, a remark that he should regret. But he was unwilling to take it back or apologize for having uttered it.

Instead, he was prepared to engage Miss Marianna Madison in battle over Seven Hills just as fiercely as he had once engaged the French, and if offending her was any means toward bending her to his will, he was quite prepared to do so.

Marianna stared at him, unable at first to believe her ears. Then the relentless color crept over her cheeks until she felt as if her face were on fire.

Without a word she turned on her heel and set off again at a furious pace, supremely conscious of Rick beside her, leading his horse along as if they were engaged in nothing more than an afternoon stroll along the Thames.

She cleared the grove of trees at the top of the drive and emerged into the clearing to see that a very smart carriage was drawn up at the front door. Her step slowed.

"Are you expecting guests?" asked Rick, at her side.

Without a word or a glance in his direction, Marianna swept into the house. She discarded her bonnet and gloves on a nearby table and opened the door to the first room that gave off the hall.

There, in a small sitting room still draped in Holland covers, stood Isabelle Madison.

Five

Isabelle Madison was dressed most becomingly, from the lush velvet neckline of her driving coat to the hand-embroidered hem of her gown. Her hair was perfectly coiffed beneath a cunning little tricorn hat that sported a yard of trailing silk. She was inarguably an attractive woman, but when she smiled, she passed the bounds of attractiveness and entered the realm of true beauty. She directed that smile first at Marianna and then Rick, who followed Marianna into the room and paused just inside the door.

She held out two exquisitely gloved hands and floated toward Marianna, exclaiming, "There you are, dear cousin! I wondered where you had got to. Dearest goose, I would have driven you here, but you ran off so impetuously." Her green eyes innocently swept over Rick from head to foot. "But tell me, who is this?"

Marianna was not a naturally suspicious person, but she could scarcely account for the change in Isabelle Madison's behavior. She was certainly behaving in a far more gracious manner than she had earlier at her uncle's home.

Still, Marianna performed the introductions, saying, "Mr. Beauleigh, this is my cousin, Isabelle Madison. Miss Madison, may I present—"

"Mr. Beauleigh?" Isabelle cut her off and moved toward Rick, her hand outstretched. "Now, why does that name sound so familiar to me?"

Marianna refrained from mentioning that the name was probably familiar because she had spoken it to Isabelle little more than an hour before. Instead, she watched with fascination as Isabelle touched one long, delicately tapered, gloved finger to the corner of her full lips.

Isabelle appeared to give her question no small amount of thought, then smiled brilliantly up at Rick. "Of course! It is *Major* Beauleigh, is it not? You served in the Peninsula and were decorated. Cousin Marianna, we are in the presence of a true hero. I am quite overcome!"

Marianna blinked. "What do you mean, a hero?"

Isabelle cast her a pitying look. "Darling cousin, Major Beauleigh is our nation's sweetest plum! Surely you have heard the accounts of his exploits in Spain—his adventures and heroism have been lauded in every newspaper in the land."

Marianna shot Rick a look of burning inquiry. He was standing off to one side, staring back at her with frowning concentration.

"Is this true?" she asked.

"It's true I served on the Peninsula," he replied vaguely.

"You are too modest, sir!" exclaimed Isabelle with a tinkling laugh. "And please forgive my little cousin. I'm afraid she's rather unschooled in—oh, so many things," she added, with an all-encompassing wave of her hand.

Marianna felt the blood pouring into her cheeks, not from embarrassment, but from the realization that she had been utterly betrayed. She had thought Isabelle would help her. She believed Isabelle would arrive at Seven Hills in the guise of an avenging angel to ask—nay, to demand!—that Rick Beauleigh leave at once. Instead, she had arrived to fawn over the man with sickening sweetness. Too late did Marianna recall Isabelle's reaction when she had mentioned Rick's name. Oh, Isabelle had recognized it the moment Marianna had uttered it, and had no doubt formulated her plan right then and there before Marianna had even left her drawing room. Isabelle Madison had come to Seven Hills not to champion Marianna, but to win Rick Beauleigh.

It was all too much. It took every bit of willpower Marianna possessed to keep from screaming in temper and ordering Isabelle from the house.

She watched with mounting fury as Isabelle placed one of her softly gloved hands on Rick's arm. "You must not think me impertinent if I tell you that the Madisons are the leading family in the area—although not, of course, on the same rung of society's ladder as your esteemed family, Major Beauleigh. I say this only because I would deem it an honor if you would allow me to take you about, introduce you to one or more of those with whom you will feel most comfortable, and perhaps—dare I ask?—give a small party in your honor."

Marianna waited for Rick's reaction, waited for him to cock that dark brow of his as she had seen him do with her and politely decline Isabelle's offer. Instead, she saw his smile for the first time, and it was a smile directed at Isabelle.

"You are very generous, Miss Madison," he said. "I cannot think of anything that would please me more."

There was something about his tone, or perhaps it was the manner in which he looked down at Isabelle, that made Marianna wonder who was pursuing whom. They certainly appeared to be a perfect match; both were avaricious and willing to do anything or use anyone to get what they wanted.

She heard Rick offer to escort Isabelle to her carriage, and she seized the opportunity to utter a rather strangled goodbye. She fled the house in the opposite direction and went across the lawns, unheeding of her destination, thinking only that she wanted to get away from Seven Hills, from Isabelle, and most of all, from Rick Beauleigh.

She set off at a brisk pace, spurred by conflicting emotions. She gained a stitch in her side, but still she continued to walk, and only stopped at last when she realized that she had dispelled a good deal of the anger that had driven her furied steps.

When at last she did stop, she gazed about to discover she had gone far afield to a quiet place of seemingly endless green lawn with only the house and stables of Seven Hills visible in the distance. It was a fine afternoon, without a cloud in the sky, and the air was sweet with the fragrance of spring grass and new buds. She rested there a moment and would have lingered longer, had she not spied in the distance a figure on foot, heading in her direction.

It was Mr. Beauleigh. She was certain of it, just as she was certain she had no desire to speak to him or hear of his military exploits or any other horrid topic he would care to broach.

She was faced with two choices: return to the house and thereby encounter him for certain, or continue on and hopefully avoid his presence. She chose to continue on.

Marianna hitched her skirts up to scramble over a gate and began to climb the broad hump of a hill. She reached the top and gazed out upon a magnificent view of rolling countryside.

How aptly the estate was named, she thought. How lovely it was and how much she wished to keep the place as her own and live there forever. And so she would, were it not for the man she watched advancing steadily toward her from the distance. He was coming out to see her, to talk to her, possibly even to gloat, and she wished with all her being he would turn about and go back the way he came.

He didn't, of course, but continued on, skirting around the meadow, steadily approaching the hill.

Even from afar she could detect the slight hitch in his step. As much as she disliked him at that moment, she knew she hadn't the heart to force him to climb all the way up the hill, not with the way he was favoring his injured leg. Slowly, reluctantly, she descended the hill to meet him.

When they were at last face-to-face, she scowled at him, and said, without preamble, "You might have warned me. You might have told me who you were."

"Would it have made a difference?" he asked, his brow flying with a mixture of curiosity and amusement.

"No!"

"Then, there was no foul, was there? Come, Miss Madison, you cannot hold it against me simply because I served my country."

"Many men serve their country," she retorted. "Not all men have their triumphs described to the public at large."

"Would you believe me if I told you my military career was not as glamorous as Isabelle Madison made it sound?"

"I very much doubt I would believe anything you had to say," she said, with frigid hauteur. "But you might start by telling me why you followed me out here just now."

He ignored her question and studied her a moment. She was without a bonnet, and the sun was shining on her black hair, lending it mysterious blue lights. There was a healthy color in her cheeks from the fresh air and the exertion of her walk, and her eyes were as blue as the cloudless sky overhead.

When he didn't answer, she said challengingly, "Well? Did you follow me or didn't you?"

"I did, but my reason for doing so has altered. What I came up here to say is no longer important."

"Meaning you came up here to gloat," she accused. She thought of Rick's smile as he looked down at Isabelle, of Isabelle laying her hand on his arm as if she had every right to do so. It was almost as if the two of them were in league with each other from the moment of their meeting. Surely by now Rick Beauleigh had convinced Isabelle to side with him in the question of Seven Hills. How could she combat them both? How could she ever win against their combined forces?

Dismally, she pushed past him, saying, "I haven't yet inspected all the rooms of the house and must go back now. You'll excuse me, I know!"

"I'm prepared to apologize, if that makes any difference to you at all."

She spun around to face him. "How gallant of you, since doing so won't cost you anything."

She was being a good deal more prickly than he had given her credit for. "I'm quite sincere," he said, taking a few steps to close the distance between them. "Marianna, what I said to you before about sleeping arrangements—it was wrong of me. I'm sorry."

She wished he hadn't reminded her, for she had only to recall his words to feel the heat of embarrassment flood her cheeks. She also wished he weren't standing quite so close upon her. If she turned even slightly, she would be able to feel her shoulder brush against the brocade of his waistcoat. Looking up into his tanned face, she saw that his eyes were gleaming—with what emotion, she could not tell, but she rather guessed it was mockery. As indignation swelled within her, his expression changed, and he smiled slightly, not in a malicious manner, nor in the manner in which he had smiled at Isabelle; it was instead a rather engaging smile that she might have thought charming under any other circumstance.

"You really don't trust me, do you, Marianna?" he asked.

"Should I?"

"Probably not. I'm a rather ruthless campaigner, you know. Too many years of military service have made me single-minded. When I want something, I take it, much as a soldier takes a piece of land, or a building, and claims it for his cause. I want Seven Hills, Marianna. I'll have it, at any cost."

It was needless for him to tell her so, for she had already determined him to be a formidable adversary. He wasn't about to give up Seven Hills, but then, neither was she.

"Thank you for the warning," she said stiffly. "You'll understand, I'm certain, what my answer must be the next time you ask me to trust you."

He threw back his head and laughed. "Very well said, Miss Madison. We shall see if you change your mind once you realize you cannot rely upon your cousin to help you. It shouldn't cause me too great an effort to bring Isabelle Madison about to my way of thinking." His smile faded slightly, and he cocked one brow as his gaze swept speculatively over her. *"En garde*, Marianna?"

Her bosom swelled with indignation. *"En garde!"*

She set off again toward the house without another word, deeply aware of Rick's presence at her side, and wondering over the prudence of having declared war against a man she suspected to be more cunning and possessed of a better arsenal than she.

They were nearing the house when she caught sight of Robin running toward them from the direction of the stables. "Hello, Marianna! I've been looking everywhere for you. What are you and Mr. Beauleigh doing out here?"

"Merely enjoying the scenery," she said in a light tone. "Mr. Beauleigh and I were simply admiring the view from that little hill over there."

Robin peered about. "It is pretty, isn't it? Perhaps one day you'll write a poem about it."

Rick looked up, his attention arrested. "A poem?"

"Yes, Marianna writes them. Whenever she disappears, that's what she's doing. Sometimes she reads them to us. Her poems are very good, you know."

Flushing to the roots of her hair, Marianna waited for Rick to make some horrid comment, but he said nothing. A quick glance discovered his gaze upon her, a speculative light in his eyes, but there was no trace of that mocking gleam she had come to expect in his expression.

Robin suddenly clasped her hand and gave it a tug. "Come to the stables, Marianna, and see Mr. Beauleigh's horse."

"I've seen it," she said, wishing to escape.

"Yes, but you haven't seen it since I groomed it. He had mud on his legs, you see, and Mr. Beauleigh let me lead him around to the stables and give him a good brushing. Only come and see him now, Marianna!"

She could have groaned aloud as a sudden vision swam before her eyes of ten-year-old Robin single-handedly injuring in a matter of minutes the magnificent animal she had seen Rick riding earlier. But she didn't pull away; instead, she allowed him to lead her around to the entrance of the building.

"He's back here!" said Robin, showing the way to the far end of a row of stalls. Rick's horse was tethered in the last stall, and a boy of Robin's age and height was on its bare back, plying a brush to its neck.

"Hello," said Rick, removing his coat and rolling up his sleeves to reveal tanned, well-muscled arms. He picked up a second brush and glanced at the boy astride the horse. "Do I know you?"

"That's Jemmy, sir," said Robin, with less than perfect manners. "He's my new friend and he doesn't have a lot to say, but he knows ever so much about horses."

"Does he, now? He must have quite a bit of experience, then," he remarked casually, as he began to ply the brush along the horse's shoulder.

Jemmy's attention was focused solely on the horse, but at this, he cast a quick, nervous glance at Rick and muttered, "Here and there, sir."

Rick ran a quick eye over the boy. Jemmy's dress was poor, and his clothes were patched. His hands and face appeared clean, but there was dirt under his nails, and his shoes were barely whole. He was too young to have his growth yet stunted by scant food and short sleep, and he wasn't gauntly thin, as were many of the boys who shared his fate. In London, a gutter-devil such as Jemmy would have earned no more than a mere glance, but in a village such as this, in a neighborhood such as the one surrounding Seven Hills, Rick felt certain Jemmy would be rather well known. Perhaps someone was feeding the lad; perhaps one of the neighbors was providing a place for the boy to sleep.

A casual glance at Marianna's expression assured Rick that she had no notion of the boy's true situation in life. She simply watched for a moment, then asked, "I do hope you boys are being careful. Don't you think you have brushed enough, Robin? In another minute you shall have worn the poor animal's hair away."

"Jemmy says a horse like this needs a hearty brushing after a ride," said Robin.

"And what else does Jemmy say?" asked Rick.

"He said your horse is a-a high-bred 'un!" Robin said with enthusiasm, "and I must agree, sir. Why, I've never

seen a more beautiful animal. Have you any others and
are they all as tidy as this?"

"I have several others, and I expect they shall begin
arriving tomorrow, along with my groom and carriages."

Robin looked up at him with approval. "Carriages!
Have you a phaeton, sir? The high-perch sort I've seen
in pictures?"

Rick cocked a brow in his direction. "Will a racing
curricle do?"

"I should say it will! And what sort of horse do you
use to draw it?"

"I use a pair. Matched grays, as a matter of fact, just
about the color of your sister's eyes."

Robin drew a deep breath of appreciation. "If ever
there was such a turnout! I—I don't suppose you would
consider taking me up in it—just so I could see what it
was like, mind. I've never been in such a vehicle nor
known anyone who owned one!"

"That might be arranged. And I should be pleased if
Jemmy would ride with us, as well."

"He most certainly will! Did you hear that, Jemmy?
We're to ride in a racing curricle. Sir, did you say it will
be here tomorrow?"

"I did, but before we concentrate on curricles, suppose
we finish caring for this horse? I was just about to put
him out at grass."

Robin stepped forward eagerly. "Jemmy and I can lead
him out for you, sir. There's a meadow just over the first
rise, if that's all right."

"I think it shall do very well, and since you both seem
to be possessed of vast experience, I shall leave him in
your hands. You'll call me, I know, if there's any trouble."

Marianna, listening to this conversation in gathering
resentment, waited only until the boys had happily led

the animal away before saying indignantly, "You cannot mean to bring your horses and carriages here!"

He looked at her in mild surprise. "Certainly I do. Why shouldn't I?"

"Because you cannot simply move your possessions into Seven Hills!" she retorted.

"I don't see any reason why I may not—you certainly have."

She flushed angrily. "My possessions can be fitted in the back of a cart! They certainly will not fill an entire stable and carriage house. And how are we to manage the upkeep of such things?"

"My dear Miss Madison," he said wearily, "it was never my intention that you should bear the expense of my horses and carriages. What a very cur of a fellow you must think me."

"I'm merely being cautious. I have to think of these things, you know, and—"

"No, you don't have to," he interrupted mildly. "Perhaps you've been too long caring for others that you've begun to believe that everything is your responsibility. It's not, you know."

She faltered, unsure how to reply. She distrusted the gentle note in his voice, yet at the same time found herself beguiled by it. There was something about Rick Beauleigh that made her feel defensive and vulnerable, when she had never had cause to feel so before. Instinct told her that he was a much more dangerous man than she had yet given him credit for.

Six

Marianna counted out the last of her precious coins and handed them to Miss Blessington.

"Never fear, Miss Marianna. I'll be quite frugal, as always, and where I can get credit, I'll take credit."

"I know, Blessing. I only wish it could be more."

"Can't be helped," said the nurse, with typical practicality. She eyed Marianna shrewdly. "You should spend some time resting while I'm gone to market. You're not looking your best."

"I don't need to look my best, Blessing, but I do need to see to this house. I have inspected but a handful of rooms, and I'm rather afraid they're all in the same poor condition. There are scores of things to be done before we can even think of attracting paying guests."

"And many of those scores of things to be done cost money," reminded Miss Blessington.

"I know," Marianna said wearily, as she slumped down onto a chair at the kitchen table. Was it her imagination, or did everything in life seem to come back to one thing: money. It was the one thing she didn't have, but she was determined to get.

"While you're at the shops today, will you make some inquiries? Perhaps some of the merchants have children who might be candidates for lessons."

"I'll do my best, but I hate the thought of your earning

wages. You weren't raised that way, Miss Marianna, and when I think of your dear mother and father—" She stopped, realizing no good could come from expounding on such a theme.

"Please, Blessing? Will you just ask?"

"I will. I won't like it, miss, but I will."

Marianna had to be content with that much. Left alone, she made up her mind to begin inspecting the many rooms of the house. It was a daunting task, but a necessary one, if she was to open Seven Hills to paying guests. She would have to examine each room, catalog its faults, determine needed repairs, and tot up the cost of bringing the room to order.

She began her inspection at the uppermost floor and was making her way systematically along the corridor when she entered a small room that at first appeared not the least prepossessing. Almost, she closed the door, dismissing the little room, to continue on her way, but there was something about it—the color, perhaps, or the manner in which the sun fought to gain entrance through the heavily draped windows—that caught her attention.

She threw back the window coverings, allowing the sun to bathe the room in light, and discovered that the room was quite delightful. The walls were covered in a fabric of delicately painted buds and vines against a pale blue background. Small paintings of idyllic pastoral scenes and miniatures of beautiful young ladies dotted the walls. She drew the covers back from the furniture and found a chintz-covered chair and footstool, a tall chest of drawers, and a finely upholstered settee atop a hand-woven carpet. Near the window was a lady's writing table, and in its drawers were expensive papers and blotters, a cut-glass inkwell, and a signet bearing the letter *B*.

In all, the room was utterly charming and bore no signs

of the wear and decay that plagued the other rooms in the house. It was only in want of a good dusting and perhaps a polish on one or two pieces of furniture, but that didn't deter Marianna from envisioning herself seated behind the writing table near the window, looking out over the front lawn and allowing her poetic bent free rein.

In this room she could be peaceful, away from Rick Beauleigh and his horrid, mocking brow, away from the responsibilities of providing a living for her family. In that moment, she claimed the room as her own and drew a deep breath of utter contentment.

"It is a pretty room, isn't it?" said Rick from the door

She swung about, feeling very much at a disadvantage wondering how long he had been standing there and if she had unconsciously betrayed any of the things she had been thinking.

"Yes, it is," she faltered, with an eye to where he was still standing in the doorway. She didn't want him to go any farther, didn't want him to enter the room and intrude upon it as he had intruded upon every other aspect of her life. The blue sitting room was hers, and she wasn't about to share it with him.

"You look as if you belong here," he said quietly.

His tone made her a bit suspicious at the same time it set her nerves to jangling. "It's a very nice room. I— I hope you won't object to my claiming it?" Instantly, she could have kicked herself for asking his permission. After all, Rick Beauleigh wasn't yet declared the owner of Seven Hills!

"No objection at all. I'm glad to see you have found something to your liking." He looked as if he meant to say more, then thought better of it. "You've been on an inspection of the house, haven't you? You'll find the room next door occupied."

She looked at him in confusion. "Occupied? By whom?"

"By me, of course," he said, watching her, his blue eyes missing nothing, from the sudden expression of realization on her face to the betraying blush that mantled her cheeks.

In that moment, Marianna resolved that Rick Beauleigh would never again be allowed to cross the threshold of the little blue sitting room. She marched out into the hallway and drew the door closed behind her, daring him to object.

He didn't, but he did watch her as she marched down the corridor, her back straight with disapproval, until she disappeared around the corner at the landing.

She searched the house for Miss Blessington, hoping her old nurse would give her some words of comfort. She came upon her in the kitchen, her mouth set in a grim line.

"What is it, Blessing? Did you have trouble at the shops?"

"Nothing to speak of, Miss Marianna, but imagine my surprise to come back to find that man still here."

"Mr. Beauleigh? Believe me, you cannot be any more disheartened than I am!"

"Miss Marianna, he cannot stay here," she said pointedly.

"I know, Blessing, and I have tried to make him see reason, but he refuses to leave."

"He must be made to leave," she said with an authority that always spurred Marianna to compliance, but which Marianna doubted would have any impact at all on Mr. Beauleigh.

"Blessing, I cannot compel the man to leave. He's too . . . *big!*"

Miss Blessington eyed her grimly. "I've spent my life

protecting you, Miss Marianna, and caring for you and your brother, but I won't be able to protect you from the consequences of having a man in this house who isn't your husband or a relation."

"Oh, Blessing, nothing will come of it, and you shall see that you have worried needlessly. I have a feeling Mr. Beauleigh's stubbornness will not survive and he shall soon lose interest in making our lives miserable. You'll see, before long, Mr. Beauleigh will be nothing but an unpleasant memory."

Seven

Marianna passed a fitful night. Sleep eluded her for some time as she lay awake, wondering where Rick was in the house, disturbed by his mere presence.

It seemed she had only just nodded off to sleep when she awoke with a start to find Miss Blessington bending over her, giving her shoulder a slight shake.

"Time to rise, Miss Marianna," said her nurse. "We don't want to be late."

Marianna debated the wisdom of drawing the blanket over her head and going back to sleep. "Where are we going?"

"To church, child. It's Sunday."

She gave in to temptation and asked in a voice muffled by the blanket, "Oh, Blessing, couldn't we miss church, just once?"

"Not if you intend to be lady of the manor," said the nurse disapprovingly. "The mistress of Seven Hills has responsibilities, you know. Now, up with you. Any more of your dawdling shall make us late enough, I fear."

As it happened, they arrived at the church just as the doors were being closed. Miss Blessington shepherded Robin and Marianna inside, and they quietly filed into one of the pews in the back.

Marianna gazed about, taking stock of the simple chapel and listening with half-hearted attention to the

vicar. He had very nearly concluded his sermon when
Marianna spied Rick Beauleigh seated several rows ahead
of her. She had convinced herself that he was not a man
who regularly attended church—unless, of course, he
could somehow gain something by doing so—and she
thought at first her eyes were playing tricks on her. But
there was no mistaking the broad set of his shoulders or
the naturally lush disorder of his dark hair. It was him,
she was certain, and when he turned slightly to murmur
something to the man seated at his side, her suspicion
was confirmed. What he was doing in chapel on a Sunday
morning, she could not guess; that every charitable and
godly thought had flown from her mind as soon as she
recognized him, was a circumstance that left her feeling
uncomfortable indeed.

No sooner was the service concluded than she made
to hurry Miss Blessington and Robin outside, to escape
the chapel before Rick noticed them. Miss Blessington,
however, would have none of it.

"Dash off? The very idea! I've never known you to
behave in such a ramshackle manner. For shame, Miss
Marianna! And you the new owner of Seven Hills! What
will the vicar think?"

She didn't care what the vicar thought, but she was
wildly wondering what thoughts were crossing Rick
Beauleigh's mind. It was all she could do to stand on the
chapel steps and calmly shake hands with the vicar. She
managed to utter something intelligent before she moved
away, and she would have made a dash toward the gate
had not Miss Blessington paused to chat with one of the
shop owners from the village.

Marianna glanced back to see Rick greeting the vicar,
smiling, saying all the right things. He introduced the
vicar to the gentleman who had sat beside him in church
and did so, she noted, with grace. How easily things came

to him, she thought uncharitably. He had only to walk through life, taking what he wanted, discarding what he had used, heedless of the damage he left behind.

A clutch of people gathered about him, looking up into his darkly handsome face with smiles and good wishes. Every last one of them, it seemed, had succumbed to his insidious charm. She could hear them welcoming Rick to the neighborhood, asking after his health, begging him to give their regards to his family. If only they knew, she thought with a swell of indignity. If only they might gauge his true character, they wouldn't be so quick to court his good opinion.

Too late did she realize she was staring at him. He turned and caught her eye. His dark brows rose. With his friend beside him, he walked toward her with purposeful strides.

Touching his gloved hand to the brim of his hat, he said pleasantly, "Good morning, Robin, Miss Blessington. Miss Madison, may I present to you my friend, Mr. Bagwell?"

She recognized the name instantly, and her eyes flew to the face of the man she had seen sitting beside Rick in church. So, this was Rick Beauleigh's solicitor! She dipped a short curtsy, determined to dislike him on sight. It was an impossible task, for John Bagwell doffed his hat with a certain style and cast her a friendly smile.

"A pleasure, Miss Madison. I hope you won't count my friendship with that rascal, Rick Beauleigh, against me."

She found herself smiling at him, but only slightly. He might have a charming character, she told herself, and a kindly way of looking at her, but he was, after all, an advisor in the enemy's camp. John Bagwell was no more to be trusted than Rick Beauleigh was, yet she had to admit that she was pleasantly surprised by him. In her mind's eye, she had envisioned John Bagwell to be an elderly man, wizened and gray, doling out advice and platitudes to anyone within earshot. But the man who stood before her was young and vibrant, possessed of an easy manner and a pleasant disposition.

He remained with them, speaking of the weather and the vicar's sermon, until they moved together as one toward the gates. Mr. Bagwell held out his hand, saying, "I hope you'll allow me to call at Seven Hills, Miss Madison. Of course, I might always claim friendship with Mr. Beauleigh, but I hope to see you there, as well."

She didn't know what to make of that, and while she didn't wish to encourage him, she could hardly be rude. Of a sudden, Marianna felt trapped, compelled to be courteous to a man who, she judged, would evict her from her home without a flicker of conscience in order to satisfy the whims of his friend. Wasn't he the very man Rick had boasted could convince a court to award Seven Hills to him? Even now, she was certain Rick was watching her, perhaps hoping she would say something that would offend Mr. Bagwell and thereby convince him that she was not a fit owner for such a desirable property.

Swallowing her pride, she extended her hand. "It shall be a pleasure, sir."

Mr. Bagwell said his goodbyes, and no sooner did he climb into his conservatively sprung curricle and drive off, than Robin asked, most innocently, "Marianna, why did you not want to shake that man's hand?"

She felt the unwanted heat of embarrassment in her cheeks. Had she been so transparent? If Robin had gauged her thoughts, then certainly Rick Beauleigh had, too. She didn't have to look up to realize that he was probably watching her, one of his dark brows raised, a cool smile of disdain on his lips.

She looked at Robin and said, more sharply than she

intended, "If you have time to dawdle in the church yard, Robin, I can only suppose you've accomplished all your work at home."

Suddenly, it seemed everyone was looking at her: Robin, with an expression of confused hurt upon his face, Miss Blessington, with lips pressed thin with annoyance, even Rick, through a mask of bland disapproval.

"Come along, Robin," said Miss Blessington, as she wrapped a protective arm about his shoulders, "let's you and I go on ahead. We'll lay out our meal, just the two of us, eh?" She led Robin away, tucked in her embrace, murmuring words of comfort meant just for him.

Marianna watched them go. She had never before spoken to Robin in such a manner, and she placed the blame for her unseemly behavior directly at the feet of the man standing beside her.

As if on cue, Rick said mildly, "I know the boy is in your charge and you undoubtedly know what's best for him, but I cannot help asking: was that really necessary?"

"You're right," she said stubbornly, "I *do* know what is best for him." She set off down the road, hoping Rick would not follow her, hoping he would disintegrate into a pile of dust on the road so that she would never have to deal with him again. Instead, she found him walking beside her, matching her stride.

Up ahead, Robin had recovered from his scolding and was skipping off in different directions on the road, laughing, encouraging old Miss Blessington to race him just a short distance. Marianna couldn't help but reflect how pleasant their walk would be if only Rick Beauleigh weren't there.

"Miss Madison—" he began, only to have her interrupt.

She said curtly, "Isn't it enough, Mr. Beauleigh, that

you must intrude upon my home? Must you also interfere with the way I choose to raise my brother?"

He smiled slightly. "I was merely going to remind you that my horses and carriages will be arriving today, Miss Madison. If it doesn't interfere with the way you choose to raise your brother, perhaps you could spare him to come to the stables. He might enjoy himself."

She could have screamed with vexation. Instead, she said mulishly, "I don't think it wise to fill Robin's head with thoughts of horses and carriages and things he can never have."

"He may not own such things outright, but surely there can be no harm in his paying a visit to them every once in a while."

"Until you take them away. And eventually, Mr. Beauleigh, that is exactly what will happen. One day soon, either you or I will be forced to give up the estate we have both laid claim to, and I doubt then you shall be so willing to let Robin visit any of those things."

"How very certain you are!" he remarked. "Tell me, are you always so distrustful of those who show some concern for you?"

"I don't need your concern. I only need you to go away and let me and my family live in peace."

"Ah, yes, your family. It's expanding somewhat, isn't it?"

She stared at him. "What do you mean?"

"Your brother's new friend, Jemmy," Rick replied in a casual tone. "He was in the stable all day yesterday, and he's there again this morning."

She couldn't for the life of her make sense of what he was talking about. Instinctively, her defenses went up. "You make it sound as if there's something wrong with that. There isn't, you know. Why shouldn't Robin make friends with the local children?"

"No reason at all," said Rick evenly. He let the matter drop, but he had been given plenty to think about. So, Marianna wasn't aware that her brother had turned the stables into a rooming house for a homeless boy. He didn't care to be the one to apprise her of the fact that Jemmy had taken up residence in the stables at Robin's invitation. Instead, he said mildly, "You know your brother would like to be there when my horses and carriages arrive."

"Robin has work to do," she said stubbornly.

"True, but I don't think beating rugs or polishing tables will bring the same light of happiness to his eyes as seeing first-rate horses paraded about the stable yard, do you?"

How much she disliked him at that moment! With such little effort he had made her feel like some sort of ogre who tormented children and set them to toiling at appalling tasks.

"Very well," she said stonily, "but as soon as your horses are settled, Robin must return to the house and help with the cleaning."

Cleaning was the last thing on Robin's mind as he viewed the cavalcade of horses and carriages approaching the stables. He hung back and watched, his eyes alight with the expectation of one enjoying a high treat. In all, Robin counted a chaise, a phaeton, one racing curricle and a gig, all well-sprung and of excellent construction. And the horses! He watched go by two hunters, a pair of matched grays, four bays, a singularly docile mare, and a slim Andalusian that was able, he was sure, to run as fast as the wind.

He hung back with Jemmy, not wanting to get in the way, content to watch the dazzling spectacle from afar, but when Rick beckoned them over, both boys reacted immediately.

"Sir, are all these truly yours?" Robin asked, fairly clutching at Rick's coattails in excitement.

"They are. Do you like them?"

"I should say! I've never seen such wonderful creatures."

"They stand me very well. They've all shown their mettle—not a slug among them."

"A slug," Robin repeated, taking it all in, savoring the new meaning of an old word.

"Here, let me introduce you to my head groom." Rick led the way over to where a man was standing in the center of the stable yard, barking out orders and adjuring the drivers to have a care.

"Master Robin Madison, Jemmy—this is Currant. He knows everything about horses, and he's done his best to teach me a thing or two—with varying degrees of success."

The man drew his cap from his head and nodded, but declined conversation.

"Currant, I think you should know that Jemmy has considerable experience with animals. I've watched him myself. Do you think you could use his help?"

"I don't see why not," said the groom, running an appraising eye over Jemmy. "You weren't much older yourself when first I took you in hand, eh, Mr. Beauleigh?"

"True enough. You're welcome to go with Currant if you like, Jemmy, and if you learn quickly and work hard, I shall pay you for your services."

He received no reply, but he hadn't expected one. Like Currant, Jemmy was not one to speak unnecessarily. When Currant moved off toward the stable, Jemmy followed him.

"I should like to help Currant, too," said Robin insistently.

"I know, but I promised your sister I would return you to the house as soon as the horses were settled."

"Perhaps I could come back later? Perhaps then Currant could teach me about horses, too."

"You're welcome to visit anytime, but you must be certain to have your sister's permission."

Robin dismissed this caveat immediately, convinced his sister could never behave so poorly as to deny him such a treat.

"Tell me, sir, do you ride all those horses?"

"Different horses are for different purposes. Some are hunters, some are racers, others are carriage horses."

"And which is your favorite?"

"Black Jack. He'll be along later."

"What about the black horse you were riding yesterday?"

"That was Orion, my hunter."

Robin's nose wrinkled. "That's a rather odd name, wouldn't you say?"

"You've just revealed your appalling lack of education in ancient Greece, young man," said Rick, but there was more indulgence than censure in his tone. "In mythology, Orion was a great hunter."

"Then, he's well-named after all, isn't he? And tell me, please, what did Orion hunt?"

"The Pleiades."

Robin was silent a moment, debating the wisdom of displaying any further ignorance. His curiosity at last won out. "And if you please, sir, what is a Pleiades?"

Rick cast him a sidelong look. "Women."

Robin nodded sympathetically. "Women. I'm growing up in a house full of them, you know."

"I wouldn't consider two women a houseful, but I see your point."

"But now that you're here, sir, I don't feel quite so overmatched. And if Marianna marries some day, as she claims she will, then you and I shall be left, and we shall outnumber Blessing."

The thought occurred to Rick that Marianna hadn't apprised her brother that their living conditions might be temporary, but he chose not to expound upon that topic, choosing, instead, to probe farther into a more curious matter Robin had raised.

He asked casually, "And do you expect your sister to marry soon?"

"Oh, no," said Robin with perfect equanimity.

It wasn't the answer Rick was hoping for. He tried again. "Is there any particular gentleman? Any one man who has shown a partiality for her?"

"I don't think so, although she had many beaux paying court to her before. Blessing told me so, so you must have it from her. Blessing also said that Marianna shouldn't be in any hurry to marry, but I think she is getting a bit on, don't you? After all, she is nineteen."

"I can understand your concern for her," Rick responded solemnly, "but perhaps she only appears old to you because you're so young."

"Perhaps," said Robin pessimistically. "How old are you?"

"Twenty-eight."

"When I'm twenty-eight, I shall have a racing curricle and pair, just like yours," vowed Robin.

"I have every confidence you will."

They walked up to the house together, a distance Robin accomplished without betraying any further confidences about his sister. They parted at the front door, and Rick went up the stairs to the first floor, intent upon finding Marianna.

The door to the main drawing room stood open, and inside Marianna was at work. She had removed all the covers from the furniture and had piled them in a dusty gray heap in the center of the room. Rick entered to find her at the window, standing upon a decidedly wobbling chair that shifted with her every movement. As he watched, she stretched, reaching up to the top of the draperies, apparently intent upon taking them down from their hangings, but lacking the necessary height to accomplish her purpose.

"What are you doing there?" he demanded, as the chair rocked slightly.

She turned, and almost lost her balance as the chair shifted yet again. She looked down, an expression of surprise on her face. He had caught her at a disadvantage; her hair was coming loose from its pins, and her exertions had summoned a flush to her fair cheeks.

The color on her face deepened. "How long have you been standing there?"

"Long enough to know that you shouldn't be up there. Even a fool can see that chair is about to pitch you headlong onto the floor. Come down at once."

His blue eyes measured her from head to foot, missing nothing, from the smudge of soot on her chin to the sprinkling of dust on the hem of her skirt. The look he cast her made her breath catch, and she struggled for composure.

"You don't own Seven Hills yet, Mr. Beauleigh. You have no right to—"

She got no farther. The next thing she knew she was in his arms, held high against his chest for the briefest of moments before he swung her legs to the floor and released her.

It happened so quickly, she was a little dazed, and she could only stand there, staring up at him.

He cast her a speculative look. "Well, go ahead. Rip up at me."

"I—I wasn't going to," she mumbled, flustered.

"No? How disappointing."

He was laughing at her, she knew, and she said pettishly, "If I'm not to stand on that chair, how, pray, am I to take the draperies down?"

"You can find yourself a more stable chair—a ladder is more preferable. Or you could have waited and let me do it for you." He levered himself up on the chair with his good leg and reached up, his long arms and legs stretching easily to allow him to reach the top of the draperies. He unhooked them from their hangings and allowed them to drop into a gentle puddle of fabric and dust on the floor.

He stepped off the chair, asking, "What do you propose to do with them, now that you've got them down?"

"Clean them and then rehang them. They're hopelessly out of date, I'm afraid. But there's nothing else, and the room looks bare without some sort of dressing at the windows."

"What about the furniture?" he asked, running a finger along the top of a table and eyeing the track it left with distaste.

"The furniture shall be cleaned, too. Of course, the upholstered pieces shall have to be beaten." She looked at him expectantly. "I could use some help getting the sofas and chairs outside."

"Ask Currant to help you, or better still, that man from the village who was in the kitchens yesterday morning. Either of them would be much better at those sorts of things than I am."

"Who," she demanded, "is Currant?"

"My groom. He arrived a short time ago with the horses and carriages."

"So that's why I haven't seen Robin this afternoon."

"He'll be along presently, I think, although I must warn you, his conversation will be of nothing but horses and carriages. I believe he even holds high hopes of someday riding in my curricle."

"You shouldn't fill his head with empty promises," she said, on a warning note.

"Empty? Never! I always keep my promises." He looked over at her and found she was watching him with an odd expression on her face. He said quietly, "You may have free rein of them, too, you know. You may use the vehicles and horses whenever you like."

She hadn't expected him to say such a thing. "Use them? But I—I don't think I could!"

"I see no reason why not. You cannot wish to walk everywhere when there's a perfectly good gig in the carriage house. It's yours to use, if you like. Or, if you prefer riding to driving, I have a very gentle mare by the name of Pepperpot, who, I've been told, is a most suitable mount for a lady." He saw that she was still hesitating, and said, somewhat impatiently, "You'd be doing me the greatest favor, you know. I can't drive all the carriages, nor can I exercise every one of my horses. Currant does his best, but there is, after all, only the two of us."

She was a little startled by his tone, for she couldn't think of a single reason he should suddenly be so angry. She hesitated, clearly tempted by his offer, yet unwilling to accept it. It seemed such an intimate arrangement, to acquiesce and say that she would, indeed, make use of his carriages and horses. To do so would be, to her way of thinking, an acknowledgment of their circumstances, an admission that they were living in the same house, sharing each other's property, residing much as a husband and wife would.

But they weren't husband and wife, after all. On the contrary, they were on little better than civil terms with each other. She recalled that he had told her once that he would stop at nothing to gain what he wanted, and she wondered if being kind to her was only the latest step in his plan to own Seven Hills. It would be foolish to succumb to the Eve's apple he was dangling in front of her, and the wisest course would be to thank him kindly for the offer, but decline the use of his horses and carriages. Upon further reflection, she doubted that he would accept with good grace her refusal to avail herself of his offer. The next best thing, she decided, would be to simply be polite, and she said coolly, "Thank you. Your offer is most kind."

"I'm not trying to be kind. I'm simply being practical and a bit selfish. What will the neighborhood think of me when they see the carriage house full of vehicles and you trudging about the countryside on foot?"

Although she had rather suspected he had offered her the use of his carriages for purely selfish reasons, she couldn't help but feel a little disappointed that he should admit it. She asked, unable to look him in the eye, "Do you care so very much what the villagers think?"

"No, and neither, I think, do you, else I wouldn't find you atop a chair, dismantling a drawing room less than two hours after leaving church on Sunday."

Surprised, her gray stare flew to his face. "But I didn't think it would be so very bad to clean only one room today. After all, we cannot continue to live with all the dust and dirt as we have been these last few days."

He smiled slightly. "I don't suppose any real harm may be done by polishing a table or two. You have my promise I won't run to the vicar with tales of how you broke the

Sabbath." He ran a critical eye about the room, and murmured, "This place didn't always look like this, you know."

For a moment she merely looked at him, scarcely understanding the significance of his words. "Have you been at Seven Hills before?"

"Many years ago, when I was considerably younger. I spent some happy times here as a boy."

"Did you live here?"

"I was merely a guest, but an indulged guest, I must admit. In those days, Seven Hills was glorious."

"I imagine it was, but it's been rather neglected for some time, I think."

"Decades, more like. But I daresay, with a bit of work, this house could be restored. It could be magnificent again."

She thought of all the repairs that needed to be made, of the broken windowpanes, chipped mouldings, and torn carpets, and she began to wonder if she hadn't taken on too much. "I shall settle for it being simply clean and comfortable," said Marianna. "I'm not certain a country inn ought to be magnificent."

"Seven Hills won't be made into an inn," he said, with quiet authority. "I thought I already told you that."

"You've told me a great many things, Mr. Beauleigh, but nothing you've said has made me change my plans. The ownership of Seven Hills is still in question."

"Which means that neither of us should make any decisions that might alter the place," he countered, "and turning this house into an inn is out of the question—at least for the time being."

"Mr. Beauleigh, you don't seem to be listening to me when I tell you that I shall not be dissuaded," she said, drawing herself up. "Please understand that when I insist upon converting Seven Hills to an inn, I do so not because

I enjoy being contrary. Far from it, I assure you! I should like nothing more than to live a life of leisure on this estate, with a stable full of horses for Robin to ride and a comfortable chair in which Miss Blessington may while away the days, rather than cooking in a stuffy kitchen below stairs. But I haven't that luxury, as well you know. I must earn a living, and I can see no better way to do so than to take in boarders."

"I won't allow it, you know," he said, in a deceptively mild tone. "And don't think you can count on your cousin, Isabelle Madison, for support in this."

"I very much doubt my cousin cares if I should burn the place to the ground," Marianna retorted. "She does, however, care for your opinion, although why she may do so, I cannot conceive!" It was a rude thing to say, and she knew it, but the rash words were out before she could consider them. She thought Rick would scold her, and she wouldn't have blamed him for doing so; but he merely stood regarding her in frowning silence. "I'm sorry!" she said, in a stricken tone. "I shouldn't have spoken in such a horrid fashion, but—but you always seem to say the most provoking things!"

"It wasn't my intention to provoke you, Marianna, merely to warn you off. Your cousin Isabelle is, I should guess, very much like her uncle."

"I wouldn't know such things, since I have never met my uncle. Isabelle made it quite clear he won't see me."

He looked at her a long moment, debating the wisdom of delving into matters that were best left unexplored. There was, however, something about the expression on her face, and the manner in which she stubbornly held on in the face of adversity, that made him say, rather gently, "Are you really so alone in the world?"

"I have Robin and Blessing," she said, not at all certain she understood his question, "and there are, I believe, other Madisons, although my great-uncle and Isabelle are the only ones with whom I am acquainted."

"If there are other Madisons, why do you not appeal to them for some assistance?"

"I did. I wrote to those family members I knew of—Papa had spoken of them from time to time—but only Uncle Cecil Madison responded. I daresay none of the rest of the family even knew of our existence. You see, Papa was rather a black sheep, it seems. He was forever at odds with his own father and out of league with the rest of the family. He and his father quarreled quite bitterly over many things. Grandfather always found fault, but Papa's decision to marry Mama caused the bitterest argument of all. Mama was a Trent, and while her family was very respectable, Grandfather thought Papa should aim a little higher when it came to marriage. Papa disagreed, for he and Mama were in love, and he refused to give her up. When he left his home to marry Mama, he never went back."

Venturing a look up into his face, she saw that he was watching her intently, and she could not guess what he may be thinking. But just as she was beginning to feel a certain amount of discomfort from his constant regard, he smiled slightly, and said, "You and your brother may have been severed from the family tree, but I think you may be the better off for it. Your uncle and cousin—forgive me!—do not appear the sort to allow their actions to be dictated by ideals such as love."

"You may be right. When Mama and Papa were alive, our circumstances were not plump; but we were comfortable together, and we did enjoy each other's company. I think, sometimes, that my cousin Isabelle cannot enjoy living with my great-uncle!"

"Nor can your cousin claim to hold the devotion of

her former nurse, as you do. How did you come by such a treasure as Miss Blessington?"

She laughed, and said, "She is a treasure, isn't she? When I was a child, I was rather fearful of her, for she was quite gruff and stern, but as I grew older, I realized how much she truly cares for Robin and me. We rather consider her a member of the family, and she, in turn, is impossibly good to us and fiercely protective."

"So I noticed. She doesn't like me very much, does she?"

"Not at all! If she seems a bit gruff, that is simply her way. She behaves so with everyone, but in your case, I think she is a bit wary, too. Poor Blessing, she doesn't understand why you are here, although I have tried my best to explain it all to her. She predicts disaster if you continue to stay at Seven Hills."

"Disaster for whom?"

"For all of us, but for me, especially." She laughed lightly, as if the entire notion were utterly preposterous, and it took her a moment to realize that Rick was not laughing with her.

He was merely watching her, his lips pressed in a tight line, his brows knit into a frown. "Your Miss Blessington is a very wise woman," he said. He stopped short of recommending that she pay more heed to her old nurse's advice, for he didn't think a young woman as stubborn and unfashionably independent as Marianna Madison would accept such counsel willingly. He said, instead, "She cares a great deal about you, Marianna."

"I know, and though she was never one to speak of her affections, she shows her fondness for us in other ways. Why, even now I believe she's down in the kitchens preparing our supper."

"Then, I'll go down and tell her not to plan on me, for I won't be dining here tonight."

She looked up, surprised. "Will you be taking your supper with Mr. Bagwell, then?"

"No, with your cousin, actually."

She felt her heart skip a beat. "You're dining with my *cousin?*" she repeated, unwilling to believe she had heard correctly.

"We won't be dining tête-à-tête, if that's what you're thinking. Your uncle Cecil Madison will also be in attendance. I have some business to discuss with him, and you may consider him the gooseberry, if you like."

For a brief moment, Marianna rather thought that the world had ceased to spin. Her limbs began to tremble, and her breath came to her in short, angry bursts. In a flash of memory did she recall all that Rick had said to her: his promise that he would secure Seven Hills at any cost, his warning that he would resort to any method to gain what he wanted. All these things she recalled, yet she had never supposed him to be so treacherous as to betray her in such a fashion. How he had managed to inveigle himself into Cecil Madison's home, she dared not imagine, but she nursed a fairly strong suspicion that he had done so by cozying up to Isabelle. Never dreaming he could stoop so low, she didn't quite know whether she should rage against him or simply burst into tears.

"What is it?" he asked, suddenly frowning.

She wasn't about to let him know how much he had hurt her and pulled herself together, saying, with forced lightness, "Nothing! Nothing at all."

"There was something that caused that look in your eyes just now."

"A slight headache, perhaps, but nothing more. I've been, I think, too long in the dust of this room."

"Are you very certain that's the cause? You were feeling quite well a moment ago, until I mentioned my plans for the evening," he said, still frowning. "Marianna, if

you are distressed to think I shall be sitting down to dine
with your uncle—"

"Nothing of the kind!" she interrupted quickly. "Indeed, I never gave the matter another thought."

"Marianna—"

"You cannot truly imagine that I would object to your
dining with my relatives, Mr. Beauleigh! Indeed, since
you appear to be on much more intimate terms with them
than I can ever hope to be, why should you not? I can
only hope you may enjoy yourself—and do give my regards to my cousin and uncle."

She turned away from him then, to make a great show
of gathering up the draperies from the floor, needing
very much to cough from the dust but willing herself
against it.

He didn't leave right away, but watched her for a short
time, knowing full well that the high spots of color on
her cheeks and her obvious inability to meet his gaze
signaled that she was laboring under some very strong
emotions.

Still, Marianna remained quite calm under his scrutiny,
but when he had gone, she dropped the draperies and
sank down onto one of the nearby chairs as if her legs
were suddenly incapable of supporting her weight.

Rick's revelation had knocked a good deal of wind
from her sails. Since the first day of their acquaintance,
she had thought him selfish. When he had confessed to
having a ruthless streak, she had believed him, so she
had no one but herself to blame for failing to anticipate
such horrid behavior. Exactly how he had managed to
gain entry into her relatives' lives, she didn't know, but
she rather thought she could guess at the devices he had
employed to do so. Isabelle Madison would gladly have
extended such an invitation with only a modicum of coaxing from Rick. Perhaps he had taken her hand and raised

it to his lips or held it warmly between his own, or perhaps he had slipped an arm about her waist and held her close for a moment. Oh, she could imagine such a scene so well! Certainly Isabelle would not have denied him anything under such circumstances.

Nor would Marianna. With very little effort did she recall that feeling of breathless exhilaration when Rick had pulled her from the chair and into his arms. In that moment when he had held her against him she had been aware of nothing but him, and if he had asked her for the moon, she would have done her level best to pluck it from the heavens and present it to him.

The realization that he might possess that kind of power over her was not a welcome one. Even more alarming was her awareness that Rick Beauleigh was a singularly attractive man. For the first time, Marianna saw him as she thought Isabelle must see him. An unfortunate circumstance, for in her heart she knew that no good could come from owning an attraction for Rick Beauleigh.

Eight

Miss Blessington and Robin were already eating their supper at the old oak table in the kitchen when Marianna entered the room.

"There you are," said Miss Blessington mildly. "I was beginning to wonder where you had gone to. Your supper is well on to being ruined from waiting, and you were so long, I hadn't the heart to make your brother wait."

"Sit here," invited Robin around a mouthful of food, "and taste the pudding Blessing made. It's heaven!"

The smile on Miss Blessington's lips took a good bit of the sting from her words, as she said, "Master Robin, you must eat a bit slower. Simply because we are dining in the kitchen doesn't mean you may toss your table manners to the wind."

"Yes, yes, only Marianna must taste this!" he said, holding out to his sister a spoon laden with food.

Marianna sat down beside him and took a bite from Robin's spoon. She looked quickly up at Miss Blessington. "It's delicious. Blessing, how did you come by the ingredients to make such a wonderful pudding?"

"And only wait until you have had some of the chicken," Robin advised her. "She made it with a gravy that tastes almost as good as any cream I've ever had!"

Miss Blessington ladled a serving of chicken onto a plate for Marianna, saying, "Now, Master Robin, if you were to keep your mouth busy chewing your supper rather than praising me, we'd both be happier, I think." Still, she smiled rather complacently as she set the plate in front of Marianna and began to carve off another slice from the loaf of fresh bread for Robin.

"I'd say this is the best meal we've ever had, wouldn't you, Marianna?" asked Robin. "It's ever so much better than the cold food we've been eating the past few days."

"The meal is delicious," she answered, having sampled a bit from every dish on the table. "You must tell me how you managed all this, Blessing. The shops must have given us credit, after all."

"Not credit, Miss Marianna. There was no need, you see. Not when I was able to pay then and there for everything we needed. I made quite an impression on the shopkeepers, I can tell you, and very happy they were to have my business."

Marianna looked up, a question in her eyes. "You paid for all this?"

"Indeed I did," she answered, busily making a fresh pot of tea.

"But the money I gave you was so little. How were you able to stretch it to purchase so much?"

"I wasn't called upon to stretch, Miss Marianna, for a bit was added, you see. Mr. Beauleigh gave me some money to use, as well."

Marianna sat very still, the food on her plate suddenly forgotten. "Blessing, you didn't! Tell me you didn't accept money from Mr. Beauleigh!"

"Lord love you, child, of course I did. The money you gave me, as precious as it was, wouldn't have fed a cat, let alone you and your brother, and Mr. Beauleigh, besides."

"Oh, Blessing, how could you?" cried Marianna, almost moaning.

"Now what have I done to set you off so?"

"You accepted money from—from that man! It was wrong of you. Horribly, terribly wrong!"

"Well, this is fine weather for ducks!" exclaimed Miss Blessington in some disgust. "After I've worked all day to put the first decent food in you and your brother in over a week—! I never dreamed I should receive a scolding for wishing to see the two of you well fed!"

"I'm not questioning your motives, Blessing, but I am questioning Mr. Beauleigh's! Don't you see what he has done? He knows our circumstances very well and thinks to gain an advantage over us by—by—! Oh, I don't know how he means to do it, but I know that somehow he shall twist it about so he can take Seven Hills away from us. I tell you, he's not to be trusted."

"No, Marianna! That isn't true," Robin said, deeply distressed. "Mr. Beauleigh is very kind and he lets me help with the horses and tomorrow I shall ride in his curricle. He's kind, truly he is!"

"Now see what you've done?" Miss Blessington demanded. "You've upset your brother needlessly."

"I shall explain everything to Robin, thank you," she retorted hotly, "although I wouldn't have to make explanations if only that man had never come into our lives!"

"If you took a moment to listen to yourself, I think you'd agree that you sounded quite foolish just now." Miss Blessington poured out the tea, and in her agitation, she uncharacteristically allowed some of it to slosh out of the cups and onto the scrubbed table.

A flush of embarrassment mixed with anger rushed to Marianna's cheeks. She said, rather haltingly, "You are not to accept money—nor anything else—from Mr. Beauleigh, Blessing. Nothing at all. I—I forbid it!"

Miss Blessington set the teapot down on the table with a clatter and said through tight lips, "I've never spoken to you in anger before, Miss Marianna, and I don't suppose I shall begin to do so now."

She left the room without another word, and Marianna and Robin sat in silence for some moments, their eyes upon the door, as if they expected she would return to them directly.

After a moment Robin said, rather anxiously, "Marianna, why would Mr. Beauleigh want to take our home away? Why would he, Marianna?"

"Robin, dear, I'm afraid there are a great many things you're too young to understand."

"He wouldn't hurt us, Marianna. Truly, he wouldn't!"

She didn't like seeing him so distressed, and said, in a comforting tone, "I'm certain you are right. Perhaps it's all just a misunderstanding. Now, why don't you finish your supper, dear?"

"Oh, I'm finished, I think, although you've hardly eaten anything at all."

"I guess my appetite isn't what it should be."

"You aren't truly angry with Blessing, are you, Marianna?"

"Only a little, but I expect we shall be right as rain by morning. You mustn't refine too much upon our little argument, you know." She put her arm about his slim shoulders and gave them a slight squeeze. "Don't you worry, Robin. By tomorrow all will be forgiven, and we shall be just as we were, you'll see. Now, why don't you go up and prepare for bed while I clear the table?"

"May I help?" he asked.

She was about to begin gathering up dishes, but at this her head swung about. "May you *what?*"

"May I help you clear the table?"

In the past, Marianna had often charged her brother with household tasks, but it wasn't in his nature to offer to do more than was required of him. "You're very kind to offer, Robin."

He smiled and said, "Oh, I mean to be more of a help to you now, Marianna. It isn't fair that you should carry the burden for all of us."

"Why, Robin, I didn't know you felt that way," she said tenderly.

"I didn't until Mr. Beauleigh put me in the way of it. He said he didn't think you ever had any fun in life because you were forever worried about caring for everyone else."

The tender sentiments that she had been nursing rapidly changed to indignation as she was faced with yet another example of Mr. Beauleigh's interference in her life. She said slowly, "I see. I hope in the future you will remember that it is impolite to discuss your sister with a veritable stranger."

"Mr. Beauleigh's not a stranger, Marianna. Not now. Not after we've known him for *two days!*"

She didn't think any good would come from arguing with the logic of a ten-year-old boy. "Robin, you must promise that you won't discuss our situation with Mr. Beauleigh. He's a very busy man, and he has very important things on his mind. You mustn't bore him with our troubles, and you must certainly not discuss with him whether or not I have fun in my life."

"But if I may not speak to Mr. Beauleigh, he won't allow me to ride in his curricle."

"Robin, dear, I haven't forbidden you to speak to Mr. Beauleigh. I am only asking that you limit the topics of your conversation to other than your family. Speak of horses and carriages and your friend, Jemmy, but do not speak of our circumstances, and especially do not speak of me."

He gave her words some thought. "Very well, I shall do my best. Now, shall I help you or not?"

"There's no need, but your offer pleased me very much, Robin, dear. Instead, I think you should go up to your room as I asked. I shall come to you presently."

She thought he had obeyed her, but when next she turned around to gather up more dishes, she discovered that Robin had heaped a serving of chicken upon his dinner plate and was making his quiet way toward the door.

"Robin? What on earth are you doing?"

He turned about reluctantly, and his face was flushed with embarrassment. "I was merely thinking that I might be hungry in the night and wouldn't wish to wake you or Blessing, so I thought I should just have a bit of food next to my bed, in case I need it."

"You'll do nothing of the sort, young man. If you're hungry, you shall sit right back down at this table and eat."

"But, Marianna, I'm not hungry *now*, but I might be *later*," he said, quite patiently.

"If you are hungry later, you may wake me and tell me so, but you are not to take food from this kitchen," she said sternly.

Robin reluctantly handed his plate to his sister.

"Now up to bed," she ordered, and watched long enough to assure herself that when he left the kitchen, he turned toward the direction of the stairs that would take him up to the bedchamber they shared. She firmly suspected that Robin, given the chance, would turn toward the stables, rather than his bed. The fact that he had grown quite horse-mad was yet another wrong she could lay at the door of Rick Beauleigh. He had caused her to argue with her old nurse, too—a circumstance that brought her a good deal of distress—and she knew that they never would have come to such a pass had Rick not interfered in their lives.

She heard the door open and looked about, thinking Robin had returned with yet another complaint in the hopes of delaying his bedtime. But it was not Robin who stood just inside the door, but Miss Blessington. She went directly to the table and took up some of the dishes, saying, "I've come to clear away the table, Miss Marianna. It's not right that you should be doing such work."

Marianna felt a sudden fullness in her throat. She put a hand on her nurse's arm, and said, "Blessing! I'm so glad you have come back! No, no, leave those things for now, and let me tell you how sorry I am. I should never have spoken to you as I did! I—I was wrong."

"Lord love you, Miss Marianna, you don't have to tell me that."

"Oh, yes, I do," she said, believing that she couldn't rest easy until she had confessed all. "I behaved horridly to you and I can't think why I did it."

"Can't you, child?" asked Miss Blessington mildly.

"As a matter of fact, I was thinking before you came in just now that this entire evening was the fault of Mr. Beauleigh. He truly is a beastly man, Blessing, and because of him, I alienated you, I distressed poor Robin, and I acted like a petulant schoolgirl. Oh, how I wish that man had never set foot in this house!" She broke off, seeing Miss Blessington's lips tighten disapprovingly. "You think I'm wrong, don't you?"

"Not wrong, Miss Marianna, just mistaken. I don't like hearing you speak so of Mr. Beauleigh, especially when he's been so kind."

"Kind? Is that how he seems to you?"

"Yes, and he seems that way to Master Robin, too, I think. Tonight at supper he was full of talk of Mr. Beauleigh and Currant. I daresay your brother thinks the sun doesn't rise in the morning until Mr. Beauleigh wakes up. And as long as we're on the subject, I might as well tell you that he's been kind to me and to you, too, if you'd only consider."

She almost gasped. "Blessing, you cannot mean it! Why, if only you knew Mr. Beauleigh as I do, you wouldn't say such things! If you knew what he was doing at this very moment—!" She broke off, flustered, as a vision rushed to her mind's eye of Rick Beauleigh with Isabelle Madison, his dark head bent toward hers, his arm possessively about her, murmuring tender words that might convince her to use her influence to ensure Seven Hills would go to him. It was a horrid vision, one that provoked a good deal of resentment and a niggling of another emotion she refused to name.

"Miss Marianna, I won't argue with you anymore, but I will say that if we must live together in this house, you might be a bit more civil to the man."

She bit back a hasty retort and counted to ten as Miss Blessington had taught her to do years ago. "You know, just this afternoon Mr. Beauleigh told me you were a treasure."

"Did he now? Why would he think such a thing, I wonder?"

"Why, indeed?" she asked archly, and planted yet another kiss on her nurse's cheek.

"That will do, Miss Marianna. Now, suppose you go on about your business while I finish clearing up."

Marianna protested, insisting she would stay and help, but in the end Miss Blessington's will proved stronger. Dismissed from the kitchens, Marianna retreated to the little blue sitting room, the place she had claimed as her sanctuary, and sat down at the writing table, intending to work on a poem she had begun some days before.

Her mind refused to concentrate on the verse, preferring to dwell instead on the little dinner party at Madison House. She had the odd notion that her fate, and the future of her brother and nurse, was being decided in the Madison dining room. If she knew Rick Beauleigh—and she rather thought she had judged his character to a nicety—he would by now have steered the dinner conversation to the topic uppermost in his mind: the ownership of Seven Hills. By now, too, he would have plied his wiles against Cecil Madison with the same cunning he had used with Isabelle. In the end, he would get what he wanted—of that she had no doubt—and she, Robin, and Miss Blessington would have to seek a new place to live. She should have been frightened by the prospect; she found, instead, that she was profoundly disappointed. Mr. Beauleigh had warned her that he was an adversary to be reckoned with, but she hadn't taken his words to heart. Now she knew better, but it was probably too late. The damage was done, and Rick Beauleigh was to have his way.

She was still dwelling on this melancholy prospect when she heard the door to the next room open then close. A quick glance at the clock told her that the hour was late. She heard Rick moving about in his room, preparing for bed. Churlishly, she supposed he would have no trouble falling asleep. She had read somewhere that a man possessed of a criminal mind often had the capacity to sleep quite peacefully, unaware and uncaring of his crimes or the harm they inflicted. The fact that he was intruding upon her peace of mind, invading the haven of her little blue sitting room, seemed to Marianna to be his worst crime yet. In vain did she try to ignore the sounds of his movements in the next room. When at last his movements ceased and she heard nothing but quiet, she found she still could not concentrate on her writing. Instead, her thoughts returned to Rick Beauleigh and Isabelle. And once again, that nagging feeling she judged to be resentment tugged at her heart.

Miss Blessington was already up and about by the time Marianna awoke the next morning. She woke Robin and sent him down for his breakfast while she dressed and prepared to walk to the village. She had made up her mind to skip the morning meal in order to make an early start of it, but in truth, she simply wished to avoid coming face-to-face with her old nurse. She was still feeling a bit embarrassed over coming to sword point with Miss Blessington the night before, and the memory of their argument was still fresh in her mind. How much easier it would be to face her, Marianna reasoned, when she could proudly place her own hard-earned coins in Miss Blessington's hand and tell her that they no longer required any assistance from Mr. Beauleigh.

She left the house in a confident mood and was starting down the drive when Mr. Bagwell drove up in his curricle.

"Good morning, Miss Madison! Are you on your way out? Do let me drive you."

She hesitated. "I shouldn't wish to take you away from your business here. Surely you have come to see Mr. Beauleigh."

"And you, of course. In fact, I was rather hoping to have a moment to speak to you in private. Do say you'll allow me to drive you!" he encouraged, reaching his gloved hand down to her.

The wound Rick had dealt her the night before still smarted, and she was reluctant to accept anything offered by Rick or one of Rick's allies; but she reasoned that no real harm could come from accepting Mr. Bagwell's offer. She smiled politely and reached up to grasp his offered hand, and no sooner was she settled on the seat beside him, than he set off down the drive and turned onto the road that would take them to the village.

"It's good of you to let me drive you, Miss Madison. I'm aware you were a bit hesitant, and I understand your feelings."

Being wary was one thing; being rude was an entirely different matter, and it had never been her intention to offend him. She said quickly, "Mr. Bagwell, please forgive me. It is only—"

"I understand perfectly," he said affably.

"You do?"

"Certainly. After all, why should you wish to be alone with me when I am already known to be a good and trusted friend of a man with whom you are in dispute?"

She cast him a measuring glance. "A very good question, sir."

"Yes, it is, isn't it?" he returned with a smile. "And I've a good answer. You see, you wouldn't know it to look at me, but I'm a man with a reputation for fairness and a high degree of honor. I try to conduct my business in an ethical fashion, knowing full well there are some things I cannot bring myself to do, even though I know that doing such things may gain me the upper hand. It's my nature, Miss Madison."

"I cannot imagine that anyone should wish you to be otherwise," she remarked.

"It happens, from time to time. As a solicitor, it has been my misfortune to represent people who disagree with my code of honor."

She shifted uncomfortably. "Mr. Bagwell, why are you telling me this?"

"I'm not certain, really. I suppose I just wanted you to know that you have nothing to fear from me."

"Are you telling me that I should fear Mr. Beauleigh?"

He looked surprised. "I would never speak so against

a friend, especially a friend of such long standing as Rick Beauleigh."

"Mr. Bagwell, I cannot understand your meaning," she said, in all sincerity. "If you do not wish to speak ill of your friend, why bring him up to me in such a way?"

"I can see I'm doing this very badly. I'm only trying to tell you that nothing is settled, despite anything Rick may say to you. He can be a bit intimidating—it's that military background of his! But he cannot force you from the property. Not now, at any rate."

"Thank you for telling me. It was kind of you, especially in light of your friendship with Mr. Beauleigh."

They were silent a moment. Then he asked, rather casually, "He is staying there at Seven Hills, isn't he? He mentioned to me once that he refused to leave the place. Another example of his stubbornness—he was always so, even as a boy."

Marianna smiled at him. "Yes, Mr. Beauleigh is staying there."

"In the house?"

"Yes, and excessively uncomfortable it is, I can assure you. He seems to be everywhere, intruding in every way in matters that are of no concern to him. Why, just last night I had a terrible row with my brother's nurse because of him. How I wish he would leave us in peace!"

"What was the row about, if you don't mind my asking?"

"Money," she said, with a sigh.

"The age-old problem," he commiserated.

"You see, I haven't any, but Mr. Beauleigh seems to have plenty. He gave Blessing—our nurse—a frightful sum, one that I shall never be able to repay. Even if I were to teach scores of pupils, I shall never earn enough to give the money back."

"Pupils? Are you a teacher, then, Miss Madison?"

"Not yet, but I shall be. I plan to give lessons in the village. I'm very adept at French and Italian, and my watercolors are very good. I'm certain there must be families who would wish their daughters to have such accomplishments."

"You're very clever, Miss Madison," he said encouragingly. "I trust you will tell me if I may assist you in any way."

His offer was a warm surprise. "I wouldn't wish to impose, sir."

"Not at all. Now, you must direct me where to drop you," he said as they approached the village.

He drew up at the street she indicated, and before she could get out, he shook her hand and held it a little longer than necessary. "Please remember what I told you about Rick Beauleigh," he said, casting her a look that effectively caught her attention. "He's a man who is rather used to getting what he wants and damn the cost. He sometimes forgets he cannot conquer the polite world using the same methods he utilized to bring the French to their knees."

"My cousin said he's something of a war hero. Is it true, Mr. Bagwell?" she turned and asked after exiting the carriage.

"Indeed it is. Rick was a magnificent soldier, but then, the most ruthless men usually are."

He touched his fingers to the brim of his hat and drove away, leaving Marianna with plenty to think about. It was a curious situation to find herself in Mr. Bagwell's company in the first place, but then to have him confide in her was an altogether different experience. She rather tended to believe that the things he had told her about Rick and about himself were true. After some consideration, she was glad of their encounter and believed she had made an important ally in John Bagwell. At last her life was looking a bit more stable; at last she could look with optimism toward the future. Now it only remained for her to gain an income and she would consider her morning well spent.

Marianna put on her best smile and pushed open the door of the largest and most prosperous shop in the village, certain that behind its doors rested the answer to all her troubles.

she was looking? Or more stables at last she could bear with her rising toward the future. Now it only remained for her to grit her teeth and sew while she waited for the time well spent.

Marianna put on her best smile and pushed open the door of the inspin and most important shop, at the very center of the village, and as she stood she started to all her homage

Nine

Marianna didn't leave the village shops in the same high spirit. Her mission in the village, which had seemed so promising, ultimately ended in defeat. She visited shop after shop, home after home, and was unable to find anyone willing to pay for lessons in French or Italian. Her prospects were bleak, her chances for supporting her family were slim, and any thought of raising the funds to turn the tired old manor house at Seven Hills into a hotel fairly dissolved before her eyes.

She had built up in her mind such a fantasy of herself and her family at Seven Hills, living a life of genteel ease, such as they were used to before her parents died and her troubles began. Now there was no chance that the fantasy might ever become reality; she had no income, no way to support them. She had failed miserably.

She returned home in discouragement. Walking up the drive, she looked at the manor house as if for the first time. She noted a windowsill in need of painting, a missing corbel under the eaves, and a section of roof above one of the dormered windows where the tiles were missing. The house was in need of repairs, and she had no way to accomplish them.

She entered the house through a side door, hoping to avoid Miss Blessington, for she didn't think she could bear having to admit failure, even to that longtime confidante. She managed to climb the stairs unnoticed and was just about to enter the little blue sitting room to cower alone and dwell upon her defeat, when she heard Rick's voice from behind.

"A moment, Miss Madison, if you please," he said. He opened the door to the sitting room and held it for her.

The last thing she wanted was to give him a moment, but she couldn't think of any excuse that would make him go away and leave her alone in her misery. She stepped across the threshold and heard the door latch closed behind her.

She whirled about. "Is closing the door necessary?"

"It is, since I wouldn't want anyone to overhear what I have to say to you. I intend to spare Miss Blessington's feelings, which is more, I might add, than I can say for you."

She watched him uneasily. "What are you talking about?"

"I'm talking about the scolding you gave her last night," he said, moving farther into the room. "You upset her, Marianna."

"*I* upset her!" she repeated, fairly choking with emotion. "How dare you intrude in a matter that is no concern of yours!"

"But it is my concern, I assure you. I gave her the money—"

"She told me you had," she interrupted hotly, "and for that I did scold her. I admit it freely! For we are not charity cases, Mr. Beauleigh. We are not accepting donations—especially from a man who is doing his level best to complicate our lives!"

He cocked one brow and gazed at her with interest. "And how, precisely, am I doing so?"

She searched her mind wildly and offered up the only

complaint she could muster. "You—you encourage Robin to loiter about that dreadful stable."

"He's a boy, Marianna. Where would you have him loiter—a taproom? Or perhaps near your skirts? You didn't strike me as the type of woman who likes to keep her men on short reins."

"We weren't speaking of Robin!" she said furiously, "but of Blessing and how you—you *manipulated* her."

Those dark brows of his rose again. "Now, what makes you think I would want to do that?"

"So you could give her—give me!—money! So we would be indebted to you. So—oh, I don't know why you would do it! I only know that you did!"

"So that is what's sent you up in the boughs! You're not angry because I gave her too much money—you'd rather I hadn't given her any money at all."

"Certainly I'm angry! I'm not a charity case, and I won't take anything I haven't earned."

"The only thing you've earned, I think, is a good trimming."

Her head came up with a snap.

"Don't worry, I shan't act upon it," he assured her, "although I'm fast clinging to the opinion that I'd be justified if I did. The fact of the matter is, Miss Madison, that for the time being—for good or for bad—I live here, too. I use candles in my bedchamber and drink your water and eat your food that your nurse is kind enough to prepare for me. All those things cost money, Miss Madison, and I'll be damned if I'm going to live off the meager—or should I say, nonexistent!—earnings of a girl barely out of the schoolroom. You don't have exclusive rights to pride, Miss Madison!"

Pride. She had clung to it as long as possible, only to discover that it was fast deserting her when she needed it most. After his betrayal last night and her defeat in the village this morning, the last thing she had needed was a tongue-lashing from Rick Beauleigh. She could feel the tears fill her eyes and knew that she was about to disgrace herself completely.

She turned away, hoping he wouldn't see, but it was too late. His hands were at her shoulders, turning her about, the better to look at her.

"Marianna? For God's sake, what—? Come here." He pressed a kerchief into her hand and led her over to the settee, forcing her down upon the cushions. "What is it? Tell me what's wrong."

She gave her head a small shake, refusing to speak, but when he didn't say anything after a long silence, she looked up and found his gaze upon her. His expression was concerned, even a trifle grim, as he looked down at her.

"I can't tell you," she said, sniffing slightly, "but I've gotten myself into an awful fix. There's no money and I thought I could earn some—!"

"The lessons?"

She nodded. "I went all over the village today. I almost begged one of the shopkeepers to engage me, but he wouldn't. I felt so—so ashamed."

He looked at her for a long moment. "You've nothing to be ashamed of, Marianna. You've taken on an enormous responsibility. Most girls your age would have crumbled long ago."

"I can't think what I am to do," she said on a sob. "I haven't any way to earn a living besides giving lessons, and if no one wants them—"

"I want them," he said impulsively.

Her eyes flew to his, her tears forgotten. "What did you say?"

"I want lessons. Teach me."

He was laughing at her, she was certain of it, although

his face bore no expression at all. She guessed she was simply the butt of some quirkish humor she had never before seen him demonstrate. She repeated suspiciously, "Teach *you?*"

"Why not? You're a teacher with knowledge to share, and I'm a student, willing to learn."

"Have you lost your senses?" she demanded.

"Not at all. In fact, now that I think upon it, another language would have served me well when I was with my regiment."

She stared at him, unable to trust him, yet certain in her heart that he had meant every word he said. "I—I couldn't!"

He took her hand and led her over to the writing table and held out the chair for her.

She sat down, and he drew a smaller chair to the opposite side of the table.

"Shall we begin now?"

She felt herself flushing. "You cannot mean to go through with this!"

"We're wasting time. I trust your fee isn't calculated by the hour."

She hesitated, knowing full well that she couldn't refuse him if he truly wished to learn, yet she deeply suspected that he had no actual desire to learn any language. She guessed that he was simply being kind to her, that was all, and the notion left her feeling a bit flustered and strangely shy.

She looked at him, trying to read some hint in his expression that would provide a clue to his true motives. She saw only expectation there and something else, some faint emotion that made her want to drag a simple French lesson out until it lasted for hours just so she could see that look in his eyes a little while longer.

She took a deep breath as if she were about to plunge

into unknown waters. "Very well," she said, "if you are entirely certain . . ."

Over the course of the next week, the household fell into a pattern. Each morning would find Marianna and Miss Blessington working about the house, selecting a room, then cleaning and polishing it until it glowed. Robin and Rick worked in the stables with Currant and Jemmy. Evenings found them all together in the drawing room, reading and playing jackstraws, or spillikin, until it was time for Robin to go to bed. Afternoons were set aside for Rick's French lesson, which he insisted should be conducted without opportunity for interruption or distraction. To that end, he often changed the venue of the lessons, at times asking Marianna to conduct them in the library, or her blue sitting room. But on those days that promised fine spring weather, he frequently beguiled her into conducting them in the out-of-doors. On this afternoon, Marianna found herself teaching Rick the basics of the French language while seated upon a blanket beneath the shady branches of a gnarled oak tree.

Rick proved to be an apt pupil. He learned quickly and remained charmingly tolerant of her attempts to correct his accent. Their time spent together in lessons constituted the only times when they did not end up at dagger drawing. In those pleasant hours, Marianna found herself quite at charity with Rick, and on more than one occasion, she caught herself watching him, admiring the look of him as he lounged upon the blanket, the wind lightly ruffling his dark hair. He truly was a most handsome man, and had he not set himself up as her nemesis, she might have become deeply attracted to him. She knew he could be possessed of a good deal of charm when he wanted to be, for she had seen him at his most genial with Robin and Miss Blessington, but she couldn't help but be suspicious whenever he directed his charm her way, and couldn't help but believe he did so only to further his cause to possess Seven Hills.

Still, it was rather lovely to be with him, comfortably enjoying the sweet, clear air of a spring afternoon. She was employed in the task of correcting his pronunciation of a certain word when she realized he wasn't paying the least attention. He was stretched out upon the blanket, propped up, as usual, upon one elbow, his long legs stretched out before him, his fingers picking idly at the grass.

She had to speak his name twice before he looked over at her. "Mr. Beauleigh, have you heard anything I've said in the last few minutes?"

He smiled slightly. "It's a bad pupil, is it not, who chases rainbows during a lesson?"

"A paying student is always a good student," she said promptly, "unless, of course, your daydreams were lacking in any redeemable quality whatsoever. Tell me, what were you thinking of just now?"

He was quiet for a moment, then said, "I was thinking what a remarkable job you and Miss Blessington have done with the house. I was thinking how peaceful Seven Hills is, and how good it is to spend an afternoon just as we are, right now."

For a moment Marianna could do no more than feel her heart thud loudly against her ribs. Like an idiotic schoolgirl, she was rendered breathless by the slightest compliment from a gentleman; like a fool, she was warmed by the knowledge that he merely enjoyed being with her. She scarcely knew what to say, and managed to utter, rather haltingly, "It—it is a pretty place, isn't it? But it is in such need of repair! I noticed a dreadful gap in the roof tiles above the dormer the other day. If it isn't patched, the room below shall be damaged, I'm afraid."

She waited for him to say something, even if it was only to agree sympathetically with her assessment of the situation, and when he didn't, she was a little surprised. "I daresay it would be simple enough to fix, if one knows how to do it."

"Which I do not, and even if I did, you cannot imagine that a man who balks at climbing stairs would ever consider climbing upon a roof."

It was the first time he had ever referred to his injured leg, and Marianna was a little startled. "No, nor would I ask it of you," she said quietly.

"Apply to that fellow from the village—Mr. Hendricks, was it? He may know just how to deal with such a repair."

"I was rather hoping you would ask Currant to help."

"I cannot spare him, I'm afraid, for in addition to his duties in the stables, a certain young woman has already pirated him into helping with household chores, although she doesn't think I know of it."

She smiled. "And I was so certain you would never find out! You knew all this time that I was relying on Currant and you said nothing?"

"It made no matter to me, as long as you didn't work the poor fellow to exhaustion."

"He has been a tremendous help to Blessing and me. In a very short time, I think, we shall have made the public rooms habitable. Of course, we shall not be able to redecorate them, but we might contrive to at least restore them to the way they once looked."

"I should like that."

She waited expectantly, but when he said no more, she couldn't help but ask the question that had been weighing on her mind. "When were you at Seven Hills before?"

"When I was a child, and again in my youth. This place

didn't always belong to the Madison family, you see, and for a good number of years, it was owned by an aunt of mine—my father's sister. I used to visit her. The times I spent with my aunt at Seven Hills were, I think, the happiest in my life."

"Why didn't you tell me this before?"

"Your claim to the property is just as great as mine, Marianna."

"Yes, but I had no idea Seven Hills held a sentimental value for you. All this time I thought that you insisted upon owning the property merely because—"

"Because you thought I was a stubborn man who refused to see reason? When you're a little older, you shall realize that most people are not what they appear to be at first glance."

Even though he hadn't spoken harshly, Marianna felt as if she had endured a thorough scold. "I admit I have very little experience in the world, but I'm not as naive as you make me sound."

"You are impossibly naive," he said amiably. "You are simply too innocent to realize it. And you're too proud to let anyone with experience help you with those matters of which you know nothing."

"Such as?" she asked, her chin rising to a defensive angle.

"Such as that brother of yours. He's more grown up than you know, Marianna. There are things he'd like to tell you, to share with you, but he doesn't want to add to your burden."

"As it happens, Robin and I share a very close bond. He knows he can tell me anything!"

"Has he told you yet that Jemmy is living here at Seven Hills?"

She stared at him. "What are you talking about?"

"I'm talking about the fact that Jemmy is without a

home or family of any kind. He was living by his wits and off the kindness of the villagers until your brother came along. Now he sleeps in the stables and eats catch-me-as-can meals your brother provides him."

Her first impulse was to deny such a story, but just as a hot retort formed on her lips, she recalled a night earlier in the week when she had caught Robin trying to sneak a plate of dinner from the table. The denial turned to resentment, and she said, "And you knew? Why didn't you tell me?"

"Miss Madison, you cannot berate me one day for intruding upon your family, then chastise me the next for not doing so. Besides, I was rather hoping Robin would speak to you himself. He's a fine lad, Marianna, and his heart is good."

He said no more, a circumstance for which she was grateful. She had been handed much to think about and hadn't the faintest idea what she was to do about it. She was still very much lost in thought when Rick sat up after some time and said, "I gather our lesson is over for the day. Come, I'll walk back with you as far as the stables."

For a man who had suffered an injury to his leg, he moved quite gracefully to his feet and extended a hand to Marianna, drawing her up and plucking the blanket from the grass.

Between the pasture and the stable yard were a pair of fenced paddocks, and as they approached, Marianna could see one of the paddocks contained a magnificent horse. Currant was standing at the fence, a bridle in his hands, watching as the horse gamboled about the enclosure with almost frightening power.

Even to Marianna's untrained eye, the animal was a superb specimen. Its proud, ink black head lifted and tossed menacingly, his ears twitched and his nostrils fluttered with every angry snort. He made to charge at one section of the enclosure, then flicked his head and pranced wildly about the paddock.

Marianna felt a flicker of annoyance as she watched the animal cavort about as if he were king of the stable yard. It was obviously untamed and terribly dangerous. What was Rick thinking to bring such an animal here? It was only a piece of luck, she realized, that it hadn't yet injured Currant. And when she chanced to think that Robin and Jemmy might innocently approach such an animal, unaware of the danger—! She refused to allow such thoughts to develop, but she wasn't averse to blaming Rick for the fact that a stallion was ruling the stable like a tyrant.

"What's all this, Currant?" asked Rick, resting one foot on the fence stile.

"He's on his ropes, that one," said Currant, with a jerk of his head toward the high-strung stallion. "Almost tore down his box trying to get at Pepperpot. I knew there'd be a devil among the tailors if he got his way, so I brung him out, thinking fresh air might calm his urge, so to speak."

"You were right to do so," said Rick, his eyes never leaving the horse. "You'd best see that Pepperpot is removed to another part of the stables."

"I've taken care of that, sir," said Currant. "The Jack could do with a dash, if you ask me. Just the thing to take his mind off the fillies."

"Have him saddled, then," Rick said, his attention never veering from the still-rioting horse.

"Surely you don't intend to ride him!" exclaimed Marianna. She had seen how difficult it was for Rick to ride Orion and knew that he was made to suffer a great deal whenever he did so. She couldn't imagine how much he might suffer by riding Black Jack. There was an underlying danger to the animal's personality that she recognized at once, and this, coupled with its obvious strength and impressive size, made it appear quite menacing, indeed.

Rick looked over at her then, one dark brow flying. "Concerned, Marianna?" He waited until he saw the telltale blush of confusion mantle her cheeks before he looked back to where the horse was mincing about the paddock. "As it happens, there is no need to be. Currant will ride Black Jack. He's the only man allowed to ride him in my stead."

She couldn't help but feel a little relieved, but when she saw Rick straighten slightly and extend his hand out toward the still-gamboling horse, she began to think Rick Beauleigh was living a little too dangerously.

Without thinking, she clutched at his sleeve. "He won't bite you, will he?"

"He won't if he knows what's good for him," he answered, his gaze remaining on the stallion. "Come here, you wretched beast."

Like an obedient child, Black Jack abandoned the pastime of rushing at fences and trotted over to where Rick's fist hung in the air. Less than a foot away, he stopped, then he edged his way gingerly toward Rick's hand. He stood stock-still a moment. Then his tail twitched, and his velvet mouth nuzzled against Rick's fist.

"You're nothing but a bloody hack, is what you are," said Rick, as he spread his fingers open to rub Black Jack's neck.

Despite his rather questionable language, Marianna detected a certain amount of affection in Rick's voice. She watched as Black Jack butted his long head against Rick's chest until Rick obliged by stroking his muzzle.

She was about to say more, to demand that Rick get rid of such a dangerous animal before someone—Robin or Jemmy or even Rick—was seriously injured, but the words died unspoken. There was something about the way Rick looked at Black Jack, some emotion in his eyes, that caught her attention and held it. There was a gentleness about him mixed with sadness and a rather bleak resolve. She looked at the horse, then back at Rick, and knew that the expression she had seen was somehow connected to his injured leg and the kind of man he must have been when his body had been whole.

"How long have you had Black Jack?" she asked quietly.

"He's been with me four years. He has a foul temper and a monstrous sense of humor, but he's fearless and strong as an ox. He had to be."

"Did he carry you into battle?"

At first she thought he wouldn't answer her, so long was the silence that stretched between them. At last he said, still stroking Black Jack's nose, "Yes, he did."

"But you don't ride him very much now, do you?"

"No." He patted Black Jack's gleaming neck and looked him in the eye. "Behave yourself, you blasted beast, and let Currant exercise you properly."

As if on cue, Currant came forward with the bridle. "That's the way, Mr. Beauleigh. You just keep stroking that nose of his, sir, and I'll have the bridle on in a trice."

Rick complied, not as Marianna suspected, in obedience to Currant. He watched in silence as Currant led Black Jack away.

"You have an amazing way with him," said Marianna candidly. When Rick didn't respond, she stole a look at him. His gaze was still upon the horse, his face expressionless. "I suppose you were used to riding him all the time."

"Yes, I did."

She hesitated, vividly aware that she hadn't the right to ask any more questions, to probe into his life, but she couldn't help doing so. "Has—has it been very long since you were injured?"

He was very quiet beside her, and when he didn't answer right away, she knew the discomfort of having gone too far. She shouldn't have pried so, but there was something about Rick Beauleigh that intrigued her. When the silence stretched on, she said in an embarrassed rush, "I only ask because—I thought that perhaps—if yours is a recent injury, you might simply—when you are properly healed you shall be able to ride Black Jack as you were used to, don't you think?"

At last he looked at her. Whether he was gauging her sincerity or assembling the words with which to tell her to mind her own business, she couldn't guess.

"It's been almost a year," he said evenly.

She nodded, trying to appear outwardly calm, all the while knowing that the mere fact that he hadn't rebuffed her had caused her heart to thud ridiculously in her chest.

"Well, don't you see?" she asked brightly. "That means you can only improve with time! I daresay in a few more months you shall be back to your old self, galloping across country on that horrid horse, just as you were used to."

He cast her a wry little smile. "You may very well be right."

Foolishly, she felt as if the sun had suddenly appeared. She shouldn't have reacted so to his simple smile. Nor should her cheeks have suffused themselves with gentle heat merely from the way he looked at her. She straightened away from the fence, thinking that a retreat might be her wisest course of action.

"I shall leave you now, I think. I must speak with Robin before he and Jemmy find themselves in any more mischief, and Blessing is expecting me to help polish the furniture in the dining room."

Rick nodded, a look of understanding in his eyes. "I'll see you at dinner, Marianna."

It was all Marianna could do to force herself to walk away and leave Rick standing alone at the paddock fence. She wanted to remain with him, talk with him, discover all the little inconsistencies about him that alternately taunted and teased her. Instead, she walked resolutely toward the house, willing herself not to look back, forcing herself to keep from wondering if he was watching her.

He was. His gaze dwelled appreciatively on her as she walked back to the house. She presented a rather pleasing picture, with her skirts swaying slightly over her slim figure, and her dark hair catching the light of the afternoon sun. He had always thought her pretty, and when she had spoken to him with kindness, with that note of compassion in her voice, he had thought she might not be as indifferent to him as he first supposed. She had been curious about him, but good manners had prevented her asking all the many questions he wasn't at all certain he wished to answer. It had long been his policy not to speak of his injury, having learned long ago that by doing so, he saved polite people the embarrassment of enduring his tedious description of the damage an enemy sword can cause a man's hip. He also saved himself from having to endure their sympathetic glances when at last his explanation was complete. He had never been able to abide pity, and while he couldn't recall that Marianna had looked at him so, he rather thought her artless questions had cut a bit too close to the quick.

She had no way of knowing that before his injury he had been something of a Corinthian, having been born with a natural aptitude for sport of all kind. He had even attracted his own share of apers: younger men, dazzled by the aura he cast, who vainly attempted to emulate his manner of dress, his confident step, and the manner in

which he controlled his high-couraged horses with effort-
less mastery. He missed those days and longed for the
vitality he had enjoyed and taken so much for granted.
Black Jack was the only visible reminder Rick had of the
kind of man he had once been, and now, as he watched
Currant throw a saddle over the horse's back and prepare
him for a gallop, he knew he could not ignore the longing
he felt for the way things used to be.

"Currant! Put my saddle on Black Jack, if you please."

His groom swung about. *"Your* saddle, Mr. Beauleigh?
But I can't ride with your saddle, sir. Your legs are longer
than mine and—"

"You won't be riding him, Currant, I will."

"You, sir?" he demanded, thunderstruck.

Rick left the fence and strode across the enclosure to
grasp the bridle. "Don't you think I can do it?" he asked,
a pleasant challenge in his tone. "I assure you, I can."

"Why, no, Mr. Beauleigh—I mean, of course you *can*,
sir, but—but do you think it's wise?"

"No. As a matter of fact, I'm fairly well convinced
that no good will come of it at all, but I shall do it all
the same. It's about time this wretched horse was put in
his place, and it's time, too, for me to test this leg of
mine. Now, fetch the saddle, Currant. I'll hold Black
Jack."

Currant went off, muttering something that Rick could
not hear. He returned moments later with the saddle. "Mr.
Beauleigh, if you're thinking I'm too old to give the Jack
a proper dash, you may rest your mind easy," he said, as
he buckled the straps beneath the horse's belly.

"I wasn't thinking anything of the kind and don't give
me one of your looks. It's time I stopped coddling myself
and gave my mettle a proper test. Give me a leg up, Currant!"

Ten

It was nearly three hours before Rick returned to the house, and the fine afternoon sky had long since clouded over. By sunset a light rain had begun to fall. Currant had taken to pacing about the stable yard, weighing the prudence of awaiting his master's return against the more fulfilling prospect of saddling one of the other horses and setting off in search of him. In the end, he decided that no good could come from his galloping off in search of Mr. Beauleigh when he wasn't at all certain what direction his master had gone. He had to be content for the time being to maintain his watch from the yard.

Miss Blessington had ventured to call to him for a cup of tea, but he had declined to leave his post, knowing he wouldn't be able to enjoy a cup until his master had returned.

In the drawing room, the family gathered around the tea tray, unaware of Rick's situation or Currant's vigil. Marianna poured out a glass of milk for Robin and passed it to him, saying, "I have been going over in my mind how I shall bring up a certain matter with you, Robin. I thought of being coy or even trying to trick you into telling me what I wish to know, but I abhor dishonesty and have decided I must be plain with you. Robin, tell me the truth now. Does your friend, Jemmy, have no home?"

A parade of emotions flitted across Robin's face. "Why do you ask that question?"

"Don't fence with me, Robin. Does Jemmy have a home or does he not?"

"Well, he does—to a certain degree."

"And is that home in our stable?" When he didn't answer at once, she said, "Robin, I wish you would have told me. Had Mr. Beauleigh not told me of Jemmy's situation, I wouldn't have known."

"How did Mr. Beauleigh know?" he asked, in deep suspicion.

"That isn't the point. The point is, you should have told me what you were doing."

From her corner of the room, Miss Blessington asked, "Do you mean to say that child has been sleeping in the stable?"

"Yes, and at Robin's invitation."

"But what else could I do?" he asked plaintively. "For once I discovered Jemmy had nowhere to go, I couldn't very well turn him out. He's my *friend*, Marianna."

"You should have told me."

"But you said there was not enough money to care for the three of us, so I didn't expect you would wish to care for Jemmy, too. I thought, perhaps, if I merely shared my portion with him, there would be no harm."

Marianna's heart sank. In all the times she had complained over their circumstance or bemoaned their lack of income, she had never once considered what impact her words might have on Robin. Now she was faced with the fact that he had overheard her remarks about their lack of funds and knew all too well their true situation.

She said gently, "There was no harm, Robin. But you should have told me, and together we would have made a decision that is best for everyone."

He looked doubtfully at her. "Does Jemmy have to leave? I should tell you now that I don't want him to."

"Then, you have nothing to fear, for Jemmy does not have to leave. In fact, I was rather wondering what you would think of having Jemmy in to live with us?"

His eyes brightened. "Could he? I'd like that above anything, Marianna."

She was about to answer him when a noise at the door called her attention. She looked up and saw Rick standing there.

She smiled. "I was beginning to wonder over you. We are having our tea, as you can see. Come in and join us."

"In a moment."

There was a hollowness in his voice that made her look at him again. Then she looked a third time, trying to determine if the light in the room was playing tricks on her, or if his face had truly drained of all color. His usually tanned complexion had faded to such a degree that his skin was as stark as the crisp white of his shirt that showed from beneath his rain-dampened coat. She set the plate down on the table and asked quietly, "Mr. Beauleigh? Are you well?"

"Certainly," he said, although he didn't move at all from the doorway, except to casually take hold of the molding. "I'm perfectly well, although I was hoping I could impose upon Robin to go fetch Currant for me."

She rose to her feet, knowing in her heart that something was wrong, although she couldn't quite put her finger on the problem. She knew only that she had never before seen Rick in such a state, and she was rather alarmed by the look on his face. She managed to say, with perfect calm, "Robin, dear, please do as Mr. Beauleigh asks."

Rick stepped aside to allow Robin to slip through the

doorway, and that simple movement proved his undoing. His skin went a little paler; then his knees buckled.

"Mr. Beauleigh!"

Marianna rushed over to where he had fallen to his knees. His breath was coming in ragged draws, and his skin had taken on a very pasty hue. He held up one hand while the other still clutched at the doorframe. "No, don't touch me. I'll be all right in a moment, if only I may get my breath."

Marianna crouched beside him, wanting desperately to help but unsure what to do. Thankfully, Currant arrived, quite winded from running, and knelt beside Rick, who tried to brush him away, saying, "Get away from me. I'll be all right in a minute or two—I always am!"

To Marianna, this sort of talk bordered on dementia, and she cast a startled look at Currant. "I don't know what happened! He was standing in the doorway one moment, and the next he was on the floor, as white as a ghost!"

"I know what happened, miss," said Currant irritably. "He let his head get full of ginger and took off on Black Jack. He's been gone for hours, riding overland on a horse that would jar the joints of any man, but in Mr. Beauleigh's case . . ." His voice trailed off, allowing the rest of his observation to go unspoken, but Marianna knew very well what he meant to say. In Mr. Beauleigh's case, such rough treatment could have a devastating effect on his injured leg.

"Remind me," said Rick through clenched teeth, "to give you a trimming when I'm feeling more the thing."

"Yes, sir. Now, do you think you could stand, sir, if I was to prop you up a bit?" Currant slipped an arm about Rick's back and drew him to his feet. Rick's face, which had begun to return to a more normal color, went white again.

"Miss Marianna, if you'll let Mr. Beauleigh rest his other arm across your shoulders, I daresay we might be able to get him up to bed."

Between the two of them, they managed to half drag, half carry Rick up the stairs to his chamber and deposit him upon the bed.

Marianna wasn't allowed to stay, no matter what argument she offered up. In the end she returned to the drawing room, where she sat down limply. She hadn't realized how frightened she had been until she tried to take a sip of lukewarm tea and found the cup clattering against the saucer in her hand.

The door opened, and she leapt to her feet, only to discover that it was Miss Blessington who entered the room.

"I just took a bowl of water and a fresh cloth up to Mr. Currant."

"And Mr. Beauleigh? Is he any better?"

"His color is improved, but he's asleep—almost dead to the world. Mr. Currant seemed to know just what to do for him, though, so don't you worry, Miss Marianna."

But she did. She had come to think of Rick Beauleigh as possessed of exceptional strength and an iron will. To witness him meekly collapsed upon a bed was a frightening event and one that forced her to confront a truth she had been avoiding for days: she cared for Rick Beauleigh. She scolded herself a bit, insisting that her feelings were merely those of a compassionate young woman for an injured man—pure fellow-feeling that she might hold for any injured creature in pain. But even as her mind repeated such things, her heart knew better. She cared for Rick Beauleigh. And she hadn't the faintest idea what she was going to do about it.

* * *

Marianna did not see Rick again that evening. Before she, Robin and Miss Blessington sat down to dinner, Miss Blessington took a plate of food up to Currant. She returned with word that Mr. Beauleigh was still asleep, that Mr. Currant didn't think he was suffering, and that they should expect no news until morning.

She had to be content with that and found that when morning came, she was anxious to hear any word of Rick's condition. She dressed carefully, donning her best blue gown, reasoning that if she did get to see him that day, she wished to be in her finest looks.

Before the breakfast covers were laid, Currant appeared in the kitchen on the search for coffee. Miss Blessington poured out a cup for him just as Marianna entered the room. She gave a little gasp. Her gaze examined his face on the watch for signs of strain, or worse, sorrow, that might give her some hint of Rick's condition. She saw only weariness in his expression and guessed that he must have stayed awake most of the night.

"Good morning, Currant. How is he?" she asked anxiously. "Is he improved? Will he eat any breakfast, do you think?"

"His color is back, miss, but he's still not hisself, if you know what I mean. He's had these spells before but not as bad as this. Still, I daresay he shall be right by evening—or tomorrow, at the latest."

That was not the answer she had hoped for, and it wasn't until he had gone that she realized Currant hadn't given her any information at all. She was almost desperate for some word of Rick's condition, but was careful not to reveal such feelings to Miss Blessington. Instead, she forced herself to swallow a mouthful or two of her breakfast and schooled herself to remain at the table, chatting idly of commonplace things.

Later that morning she was still having difficulty concentrating on anything but Rick Beauleigh and was idly pacing her blue sitting room, straining her ears to catch the slightest sound from the room next door. A knock at the door almost caused her to jump out of her shoes, and when the door opened, Miss Blessington was there with Mr. Hendrick.

"Here you are, then," she said, as she ushered Mr. Hendrick into the room. "I was wondering where you had got to, Miss Marianna. Only fancy that I should find you here."

Where else would she be? thought Marianna. If she couldn't see Rick and be with him, the little blue sitting room was the next best thing. At least there she could hear if he cried out or if Currant should need her. At least in the blue sitting room she would be able to hear Rick's authoritative step upon the hardwood floor of his room and know that he was up and about and on the mend.

But she couldn't very well admit such thoughts to her old nurse, and instead greeted Mr. Hendrick, saying, "Hello. Have you come to check on Mr. Beauleigh's progress? We've heard nothing, I'm afraid."

"No, miss. I've come about that roof of yours. Miss Blessington said you were worried over it, and I come to see what's what."

Mr. Hendricks climbed upon a chair and touched his calloused fingers to where a small stain of dampness had appeared on the ceiling just inside the window.

"Do you think it can be fixed, Mr. Hendrick?" she asked.

"Can't tell from here, miss." He opened the window and swung his leg over the sill and paused. He leaned out, inspecting the roof line; then after a moment, he climbed out the window and disappeared from view.

Marianna leaned out the window as far as she dared and looked up. Mr. Hendricks was above her, straddling the peak of the dormer window, poking at the roof tiles, lifting some and pushing others back into place. Eventually, he reappeared at the window and climbed safely back inside.

"What do you think, Mr. Hendrick? Can it be repaired?"

"Aye, sure, it can be repaired, miss, but some o' them roof tiles be broken and some be gone. They'll need to be replaced, and quickly, too, I should think, before the next good rainfall."

She breathed a sigh of relief that turned to a slight gasp when he named the amount of money it would cost to repair the roof. It wasn't a great deal of money—a few pounds only—but given the fact that she had no money at all to call her own, he might as well have quoted a hundred pounds and be done with it.

"Mr. Hendrick, are you certain it shall cost so very much?"

He gave his stubbled chin a rub. "I don't see how it can be done for less, miss." He watched her a moment, then said kindly, "Ye know, I saw some oiled cloth in the stables, and it might still be there. If I was to drape it over the peak and pin it down some with stones from the wall that runs along the road, I daresay it would keep the rain out until the roof can be repaired proper."

"Oh, would you, Mr. Hendrick? I shall be grateful for anything you can do."

She sent Robin and Jemmy to work bringing stone from the side of the road, and Mr. Hendrick went off to fetch the oiled cloth he had seen before in the stables. In a short time, the makeshift repair was done, and Marianna gave Mr. Hendrick a promise that she would do her best to ensure the proper repairs were accomplished.

"It won't hold," he said, "if there be a true and proper

storm, but it should keep your pretty little room dry for now."

She thanked him and walked him out to where his rickety old cart was standing at the back door. When he had driven away, Marianna walked slowly across the lawns. Before long, she had wandered over to the old oak tree under which she and Rick had passed the afternoon before. How peaceful it was there, and how easily did the memory of their time together come to mind. It was a long time before she could compel herself to dwell on a topic that did not involve Rick Beauleigh, but very soon she found herself thinking of him again. She made up her mind to return to the house when she heard someone calling her name.

She looked up to find Currant coming toward her and hurried to meet him.

"What is it, Currant? Is Mr. Beauleigh all right?"

"He's asking for you, miss. Would you come straight away?"

Would she? It was all she could do to keep from taking off at a gallop across the lawns. Instead, she fell into step beside Currant, saying, "You must tell me what to expect. Is his color good? Is he still in such a weakened state? And you must stay with me and let me know if you think he needs anything or grows too tired."

"He's weaker than he likes to admit, but he's well improved over last night. Never fear, miss. I'll stay nearby."

She paused only a moment to pick up a book from her sitting room, then hurried to the room next door. Currant held the door for her, and Marianna swept inside. Rick was sitting in a chair near the window; his feet were propped upon a footstool, and a blanket covered his legs. He was wearing a richly brocaded dressing gown, his color was good, and his eyes were on her.

"Come in!" he said in a strong, clear voice. "No, come closer. What I have isn't catching, you know."

"I know, but it is only—I shouldn't wish to upset you."

"Since when?" he asked amiably. "Don't think you need coddle me. I've asked you to visit me because I knew I could trust you to behave as you normally do. Currant has turned into an old woman right before my eyes and won't speak to me in anything more strenuous than a weak whisper. I'm relying on you, Marianna, to interject some spirit into the conversation."

"I shall do my best, but first you must tell me: are—are you well?"

"Very well," he said promptly, and was rewarded by seeing a good deal of the worry fade from her expression.

"You gave me—all of us!—quite a scare," she said, with a nervous laugh.

"Did I? You must know I hadn't intended to do so. It's an old complaint, one I usually deal with very well, but yesterday—I'll say only that I have no one to blame but myself for what occurred."

His words had the ring of an apology about them, and Marianna felt herself relax a bit. "Is there anything you need?"

"I could do with something to eat. I'm famished, but my stomach isn't yet ready to handle a meal."

"Perhaps you might be able to eat some bread and milk. Blessing could add a bit of sweet cream for taste. I'm certain she could have it ready in a trice."

"A good idea. Currant, be so good as to ask Miss Blessington for some bread and cream. And ask her to take her time fixing it," he added, with a pointed look that Currant recognized immediately.

It was a heady feeling for Marianna to realize that Rick wished to be alone with her. She was rather certain he was aware of the sudden color that suffused her cheeks the moment the door closed upon Currant.

He indicated a chair drawn close by his. "Please sit down, Miss Madison."

"Very well. I thought you might like me to read to you, and I have brought a book with me. Or would you rather we engaged in a spirited conversation as you commanded?"

"I'd much prefer your conversation. Tell me, what have you been doing since I saw you at the stable yard yesterday?"

"I daresay you know very well what I did. You cannot think to have dropped into my lap the knowledge that Jemmy was living in the stable and not think I should do something about it!"

"I rather suspected you might," he said with a slight smile. "Tell me, have his sleeping accommodations improved at all?"

"Yes. We have decided that Jemmy and Robin shall share a bedchamber together. I don't know which of them is more delighted with the plan. Robin has been quite beside himself, saying that at last he is not living in a house ruled by women. When I quizzed him and asked what he meant by such a statement, he said that there was no use explaining and only *you* could understand." She saw a ghost of a smile form on Rick's lips, and asked archly, "I don't suppose you would care to explain what he meant?"

"I shouldn't think so, but you may believe me when I tell you that you needn't worry about Robin."

"I don't."

"Then, what *are* you worried about?"

She looked quickly at him, surprised that he would have gauged her mind so accurately. She couldn't very well admit that concern for his welfare had left her in a fretful state for the better part of the past twenty-four hours. Nor did she wish to distress him by speaking of Jemmy's predicament and the cost of repairing the roof. Instead, she laughed lightly, saying, "When am I *not* worried about something? Fretting over trifles has become my one true talent!"

"Don't try to fob me off. What is it?" he asked insistently. He saw her hesitate still, and said, "If you don't tell me now, I shall have to get up and hobble all the way downstairs and have the truth from Miss Blessington."

She relented. "It's the same stupid complaint: money. I never seem to have enough of it and now, with another mouth to feed—!" She broke off, knowing that she had tried to make her words sound light, but suspecting that she had sounded dismal instead. Relating her troubles to Rick was not going to make him feel better, nor would it help him forget his own cares. She shrugged her shoulders slightly and said, with a light laugh, "It shall all come about presently, I think."

"Is that all?" he asked, somewhat impatiently. "I don't know why you insist upon keeping such things to yourself. Surely you know that you have only to tell me—"

"Tell you what? That I haven't any money? Is that what you wish? That I should stand before you with my hand out and a catalog of woes and reasons you should frank me?"

"Why not? I'm not tight-fisted—apply to Currant if you don't believe me. He can tell you I'm a generous employer."

"But I'm not in your employ," she said, drawing herself up proudly.

"No, but Jemmy is."

"He—he's *what?*"

"He's my employee. The day my horses arrived, I hired him as an apprentice to Currant. Ah, I can tell by the look on your face you don't believe me. I assure you, I'm speaking the truth."

She looked back at him with an expression of doubt in her eyes. "But why would you do such a thing?"

"Any number of reasons. Shall I list them all for you? Very well! First, I have several horses but only one Currant, and he cannot hope to care for and handle all my horses by himself. Second, I fully intend to hire a sufficient number of boys and men to see to my horses and carriages, but I won't do so until the ownership of Seven Hills is settled. Third, the boy was obviously in need of a place to sleep and some decent food. Fourth, he has a surprising aptitude for horses. He's a natural, as Currant says, and it seemed a solution to both his problem and mine that I should hire him to help Currant care for my horses."

"You should have told me of Jemmy's circumstance, you know," she said, a bit resentfully. "You should have told me Robin was sneaking about, feeding him and letting him sleep in the stables."

"His secret wasn't mine to share, Marianna. Would you have had me betray a confidence?"

How like him to twist her words about! She was of a mind to tell him what she thought of secrets and confidences, when she glanced at him and saw that he was watching her, his eyes intent, and his lips smiling slightly. The expression she saw on his face swept the quarrelsome words right from her mind, and she found herself looking shyly at him. "I—I never thought to hear you speak so."

"Why? Do you think I have no honor, Marianna?"

"Of course not! I mean, certainly—! Oh, why do you make me say the most nonsensical things!"

He actually smiled at her with almost wicked delight. "I've no idea, but I'm pleased to hear I hold some power over you. I was beginning to think you were immune to my charms."

"Perhaps I have not yet seen them," she answered swiftly, and was immediately rewarded with the sound of his laughter. To Marianna, it was a delightful sound and immediately dispelled a good deal of the tension she felt in Rick's presence.

A knock on the door signaled the return of Currant, who entered the room carrying a tray upon which reposed a bowl of bread and milk and a dish of tea.

"That's the spirit, Mr. Beauleigh. I can't recall the last time I heard you laugh, and that's a fact," he said, well satisfied.

"You may thank Miss Madison and her delightful company," Rick said, with a smile toward Marianna.

There was a warm look in his eyes that made her feel suddenly self-conscious, and unsure where to look. She finally settled upon the book she held in her lap and made a great show of smoothing her fingers across its cover, as if she could somehow press the wrinkles from the leather binding with nothing more than her tapered fingertips.

Currant set the tray down, saying, "You've another visitor, sir, who will perhaps cheer you a bit more."

"A visitor? Tell me it's not one of the locals, Currant!"

"In a manner of speaking, sir. It's Miss Madison and she insists on seeing you. She's waiting in the drawing room."

"Isabelle Madison? She'll have a long wait. I'm in no condition to go down to her. Did you tell her so?"

"Yes, sir, but I don't think she believed me. Then she asked after you, Miss Madison, and I told her you were engaged, but she said she wouldn't go away without speaking with one of you."

Dismayed, Marianna's eyes flew to Rick's. She should

have foreseen such a situation; she should have known that Isabelle would expect Rick to pay court to her. She would have expected him to call upon her, and when he hadn't, Isabelle had come to discover what circumstances prevented their being together.

Vainly, Marianna tried to extinguish a little flicker of jealousy that suddenly sprang to life in her breast. She drew a deep breath, hoping that her face might not betray the emotions that were whirling about her head. With perfect calm she met Rick's gaze. She didn't think she had perceived any instant light of affection spring to life in his eyes at the mention of Isabelle's name, but she already knew from experience that he wasn't a man who wore his emotions on his sleeve. She said carefully, "If you wish to see my cousin, we could contrive to have her brought upstairs. Would—would you like that, Mr. Beauleigh?"

He answered by making a face that instantly vanquished that jealous spark within her. "I cannot imagine the beautiful Isabelle acting the ministering nursemaid to an old soldier, can you?" he asked skeptically.

She judged that to be a rhetorical question, and said calmly, "Very well, I shall see her. Please tell Miss Madison I shall be down presently, Currant." She stood up and set the book on a table very near Rick, so he would be able to reach it while she was gone, and was surprised when he clasped her wrist and held it.

"Don't be long with her," he said, in a tone that immediately set her heart to fluttering in her chest.

With an effort she resisted an impulse to fly down the stairs and demand that Isabelle Madison state her business and leave. When she did enter the drawing room, she was determined to answer Isabelle's questions quickly and succinctly, and do nothing that would prolong their interview.

Isabelle was standing near the window when she entered, and turned about, a look of annoyance on her lovely face. "Haven't you a proper butler in this house, cousin? Imagine my shock to find your door being answered by a groom!"

"There is only Currant and my nurse," Marianna responded patiently. "Until the matter of ownership of Seven Hills is resolved, there can be no servants hired, cousin."

"It's excessively inconvenient not to have proper servants, and it is most unseemly. You should not be living in such an environment."

"I live here because I have nowhere else to go. Unless, of course, you have come to ask me and my family to stay with you?"

Isabelle flushed slightly. "You know very well that's not possible. Our uncle would never agree to such a scheme."

"Of course not," said Marianna evenly, as she took a seat and motioned for Isabelle to sit beside her.

Isabelle claimed instead a chair close by, saying, "I didn't come here to talk about your servant problem, cousin. I've come to see Mr. Beauleigh, but his groom tells me I cannot see him."

"He's ill, I'm afraid. I have just seen him, and he's not at all disposed to visitors."

Isabelle's finely arched brows came together, and she asked, in a voice of deep suspicion, "If he cannot receive visitors, why have you been with him?"

"He is ill, cousin, and not at all himself. He doesn't wish to be alone. If I sit with him, Currant is spared to go about his business."

"Has a doctor been in to see him?"

Marianna was a little surprised by the question. "Why,

no. Now that I think on it, I don't believe he asked for a doctor."

"Don't you think it would be wise to consult a man of medicine?" Isabelle insisted.

"I shall certainly speak to Mr. Beauleigh about it, and I shall mention to him your concern," Marianna said politely, hoping to draw their interview to a close. "Is there any special message you would like me to give him?"

"Yes, there is. It's the reason I came, actually, and it involves you, too. I have convinced our uncle Cecil to hold a party at Madison House. I've brought your invitations," she said, drawing two cards from her reticule and placing them on a nearby table. "I wanted to deliver them myself so I could personally encourage Mr. Beauleigh to come, for I have a feeling he might not wish to."

"Indeed? Why wouldn't he?"

"Because he's a Beauleigh, cousin," Isabelle explained, with great patience. "Because a man who has been entertained at St. James Palace as well as the Brighton Pavilion couldn't possibly wish to attend a simple country party, even if the party is being held in the most fashionable residence in the neighborhood."

"I cannot think what you mean," said Marianna, frowning slightly. "Why would a soldier be entertained at St. James? Unless, perhaps, he was recognized by the Regent for his heroism during the war?"

Isabelle cast her a withering look. "Hearing you speak so, cousin, causes me serious doubt that you are in truth a Madison, after all! Don't you know anything about society and its *habitues?*"

"You must know that my experience in that area is entirely nonexistent. I have never been among the elite of society, as you describe it, but if Mr. Beauleigh is to be held up as an example of such people, I am rather glad of it."

"Being a provincial, you couldn't possibly understand Mr. Beauleigh's position. You could never appreciate his charms as I do." She looked at Marianna, her green eyes noting the bit of lace at the collar of her gown, and the light folds of blue fabric as it swirled about her feet. She frowned slightly. "That gown—is it new?"

"Why, no, it is not."

Isabelle's frown increased. "It's almost becoming to you. You know, cousin, I cannot like the notion of your living here alone with Mr. Beauleigh. If word of your situation were to be spread among the neighborhood—! Of course, *I* would never speak of it, for you've assured me that it's all quite innocent."

"But I'm not living alone with Mr. Beauleigh. My brother lives here, as well, and so, too, does Miss Blessington. She's an admirable chaperone, I assure you."

"Ah, yes, your old nurse," said Isabelle in a doubtful tone.

Marianna perceived a mild threat in Isabelle's words, and she felt her temper rise in response. "If you are truly distressed over our situation, you might help resolve it."

"I?" demanded Isabelle. "What on earth could I possibly do?"

"Cousin, it was our uncle who created the unconventional living arrangements you deplore, and it is our uncle who has the power to solve the dilemma over who owns this property."

"What has that to do with me?"

"You might speak with him. Use your influence. Persuade him to settle this matter quickly and fairly."

"No, I thank you! I won't be made a party to your troubles. Why, I only mentioned the matter of your living arrangements simply to drop a kind word in your ear. You know how horrid gossip can be once it is started, and your sharing a home with an attractive man who is not your husband is nothing short of food for scandal. Of course, *I* am entirely in sympathy with you. But I'm also your cousin, and people in the neighborhood don't know you as I do."

Marianna, feeling her temper mount to an alarming degree, rose to her feet. "It is comforting to know I may count on your discretion, cousin," she said, with admirable calm. "I hope you will understand that I must return to Mr. Beauleigh now. He shouldn't be left alone for long."

Isabelle stood and cast her a narrow look. "I shall call again tomorrow to see how he fares."

"I'll tell Mr. Beauleigh. I'm certain he will be delighted to hear of your concern."

"I suppose I shall have to see myself out since there isn't a proper servant within shouting distance." She moved toward the door, saying, "Now, do be certain you hand Mr. Beauleigh his invitation personally. I'm relying upon you, cousin!"

"You may depend on me," Marianna assured her, but no sooner did the door close upon Isabelle, than she nursed a strong temptation to toss the invitations into the fireplace. Her better judgment prevailed, and a few minutes later she was back in Rick's bedchamber, sitting in the chair beside him, and handing over to him one of the invitations with an expression of distaste.

"What is this?" he asked.

"An invitation to attend a party at Madison House."

He looked up at her, frowning. "Did you receive an invitation, as well?"

"Yes."

"You don't sound very happy about it. I should think

you would be a bit more enthusiastic. Don't all women love to dress in their finest and attend parties and balls?"

Had he asked her that question a mere half an hour sooner, she would have answered quite promptly and quite happily, but now she wasn't at all certain she wanted to attend any party that counted Isabelle Madison among its guests. She could think of a hundred ways in which to pass a more pleasant evening than watching Isabelle pursue Rick—or was it more accurate to say that Rick was pursuing Isabelle? He had certainly accepted her dinner invitation readily enough, and if her suspicions were correct, he had taken her driving in his curricle on more than one occasion.

The truth of their relationship was beginning to nag at Marianna. She wanted very much to ask him if he spent time with Isabelle because he wished to pay her court or if he was simply using her to obtain ownership of Seven Hills. Even if she could ask him such a question, she wasn't at all certain she would, for she didn't wish to know the answer.

"Well, Marianna? Don't you wish to go?" he asked again.

"Of course I do," she said, falsely bright. "What fun to talk and laugh and perhaps dance with new friends and acquaintances. I'm certain Mr. Bagwell will be invited, don't you agree?"

"Ah, yes! John Bagwell. Are you saying you will only consider attending if he is there?"

She was a little surprised by his question. "No, but it would be nice to see a friendly and familiar face among the guests."

"Friendly and familiar? Is that all he is? I believe you have mentioned before that you hold him up as something of an ideal."

"No such thing, I assure you! I simply think he is a very kind man."

"I wonder why? You've spoken with him how many times? Twice? Perhaps three times? Can you tell so much about a man's character on so short an acquaintance?"

"I admit I do not know him well, but when I spoke to him about settling the matter of Seven Hills, he gave me his assurance that he would resolve the matter fairly and equitably."

"Oh, he did, did he? And tell me, has he kept his promise?"

There was something about his tone that made her feel defensive. Perhaps she was still a bit agitated from her interview with Isabelle Madison, or perhaps it was that unnecessary note of irritation in his voice that caused her back to stiffen a bit. She said frostily, "Mr. Bagwell seems a very honorable man, and I cannot think of anyone I trust more!"

"A happy coincidence, since it is my fortune to trust him, too," said Rick coldly. "Tell me, Miss Madison, how do you suppose John Bagwell will manage to settle our dispute in a way that can possibly be fair and equitable for us both?"

That was a question she had not thought important enough to ask herself. But no sooner did the question leave Rick's lips, than she had to admit the significance of it. Would Mr. Bagwell, in good conscience, ever consider abandoning his longtime friendship with Rick Beauleigh and award Seven Hills to her? Somehow, she could not imagine that he would be moved to do so, despite his assurances to the contrary.

"There's no need to look so shattered," Rick said impatiently, "but perhaps in future you'll not be so quick to place your trust in someone who hasn't earned it."

"I think Mr. Bagwell has earned my trust," she said,

rising slowly to her feet. "His has been the only friendly voice to greet me since we came to Seven Hills. It would be presumptuous of me to claim him as a friend, but I do know I may rely upon him as an honorable man who will do the right thing."

"Is that a fact?" he said slowly. He watched her a moment, schooling his expression to one of calm passivity, so she wouldn't know just how angry he truly was. At last, he said, "If that's what you think, Marianna, you're much more naive than even I gave you credit for."

He was using that word again, she thought grimly, and felt once more the discomfort of knowing she had failed a little in his expectations. If he thought her naive, she reasoned, then it was no small leap to believe that he considered her somewhat inane and rather stupid, too. How else could she explain his tone and the undercurrent of anger in his words? She had no notion what she might have said or done to cause him to speak so, but suspected that his injury, along with his keen disappointment in her, had combined to cause his poor temper.

The thought that he was displeased with her was rather more than she wished to bear, and she said, "You must excuse me, Mr. Beauleigh."

His brows knit together as he watched her pick up her book from the table. "Marianna?" He sat up away from the pillows and made a move to swing his legs from the footstool.

"No, you mustn't!" she said quickly. "Please don't try to get up. I shall send Currant to sit with you."

"Marianna, if I said something—! Forgive me! I didn't mean to distress you."

She gave a slight shrug as she backed her way to the door, saying, "Not at all! Why, I am not the least distressed. But you must know I have a great many things to do. I—I shall see you presently."

She left him then, shutting the door quietly behind her. She didn't see him again that day, a fact that she found as much of a relief as it was a disappointment. She was having too difficult a time knowing her own mind where he was concerned. It was more than a little curious, she thought, that when they were apart her thoughts dwelled kindly upon him, but when they were together they always parted brass rags.

On the following day, she learned from Miss Blessington that he was up from his sickbed and at the stables as usual. That news came as both welcome and disappointing; for though she knew a certain measure of relief that he was feeling well enough to haunt the stables as he was used to, she couldn't help but feel a bit apprehensive over the prospect of speaking with him as their paths crossed throughout the day. She had never been good at subterfuge and feared she would be unable to hide her emotions. Nothing, she thought, could be more humiliating than for Rick to divine that she had formed a very strong attachment for him.

Eleven

Her worries came to naught. She didn't see Rick that morning, and by afternoon, as the hour approached when he typically joined her for his daily lesson, there was still no sign of him.

Despite herself, Marianna ventured out to the stables in search of him. He was nowhere in sight, and when she asked Currant where his master was, he kindly informed her that Mr. Beauleigh had driven out some half hour before.

"Did he say where he was going?"

"I believe, miss, he was off to call on Miss Madison."

"Miss Madison!" she blurted, in hurt surprise.

"Yes, miss, and why he would do so, I cannot say, for I fairly begged him to take things easy until he was back to his old self. He'd have none of it, of course, and off he went."

Marianna returned to the house with slow, thoughtful steps. It would have been too much for her to admit that she was hurt by Rick's behavior, but she did admit that she was a little disappointed. She had begun to look forward to their lessons and thought he did so, too. It was a lowering realization that while she was anticipating their afternoon together, he was preparing to drive off in one of his horrid carriages to call upon her cousin.

Sometime later her disappointment had flared into

something akin to misery. It was now impossible for her to deny that she was strongly attracted to Rick, but she could not determine if he carried any trace of the same emotion where she was concerned. When he looked at her, or when he smiled, she could very easily convince herself that he did care. He certainly had no small amount of charm, when he chose to, but then she recalled that he was no doubt just as charming with Isabelle. Almost without realizing, she found herself wondering if he smiled at Isabelle in the same way he smiled at her, or if he tried to divert Isabelle from temper the way he had tried to avert her anger the afternoon before. It was fruitless to tease herself so, yet she couldn't help but dwell upon such questions. She was on her way to the library, hoping to divert her mind with a book of poetry, when she heard the knocker sound at the front door.

Mr. Bagwell was there, and he swept his hat from his head, saying, "Miss Madison! A pleasure, as always, to see you!"

She invited him in and led the way to the drawing room, saying, "Won't you come in here, sir, and tell me what brings you to Seven Hills?"

He waited until she had sat down before claiming a seat very near hers. "I've come to see Rick Beauleigh, actually, but I am glad to have a moment with you. Tell me, how do you go on, Miss Madison?"

"Very well. My family and I are enjoying our days here, and we hope to have many more. Is—is that what you wished to speak to me about? Has there been a decision about Seven Hills?"

"Not yet, but I expect it won't be much longer now. Are the circumstances so very bad? I've thought of you often, you know, and I daresay it cannot be comfortable for you here."

Her eyes widened a bit. "You've thought of me?"

"You sound surprised! You shouldn't be, you know. I can't help but feel some responsibility for you."

"But you shouldn't!" she exclaimed quickly. "After all, this situation was not of your making."

"No, but I hold myself responsible for not having anticipated such trouble. I've known the Madison brothers too long not to suspect that one of them was in mischief to his elbows. I should have seen this coming."

"Mr. Bagwell, is there any chance you may have a decision soon?" she asked earnestly. "As you said, the living arrangement here—with Mr. Beauleigh so close upon us—is very uncomfortable!"

"I'm sure it is," he said sympathetically. He cast her a speculative look. "May I be frank? I promise, I won't put you to the blush; but I must say something that is rather distasteful, and I fear I can see no other way than to merely say it and get it over with."

Given such a prelude, Marianna was rather hesitant to give him leave, but she steeled herself and said, quite calmly, "By all means, please speak what is on your mind, Mr. Bagwell."

"I have been asked—rather, I've been given instructions—!" He broke off, and looked away for a moment. When next his eyes met hers, he said gently, "Miss Madison, perhaps if you were given the proper inducement, you might be made to part with Seven Hills of your own accord."

That was not at all the distasteful speech she had expected. She said, a little bewildered, "Inducement? I can think of nothing that would make me leave, Mr. Bagwell. Surely you know it is our circumstance that my family and I have nowhere to go if we were to leave Seven Hills."

"It might be within my power to change that circumstance."

She truly hadn't the least notion of his meaning, but then she had a momentary thought that he was perhaps making her a proposal. He certainly had a kindly look in his eye and his tone had been gentle; but she rather thought he had a look about him that was more brotherly than amorous. She asked, a bit apprehensively, "How, exactly, would you change our circumstance?"

"I may be in the way of offering you a sum of money, Miss Madison, if you will relinquish all claim to Seven Hills."

Since it had never occurred to Marianna that a price may be fixed upon the security of having a home and her family about her, she received Mr. Bagwell's words in a rather stunned silence. Her first thought was that he had spoken in jest, but one look in his eyes convinced her that he was quite earnest and even a bit sorry. A rash and unruly thought sprang to her mind, and she asked grimly, "Did Mr. Beauleigh ask you to make me such an offer?"

He looked a little surprised, and said, "You must know that I speak on his behalf. Rick Beauleigh has given me authority to handle all his affairs."

"I see!" she said, in a tight voice. Indeed, her thoughts were in a jumble, and her emotions were in such a state of agitation that it was all she could do to keep from leaping from her chair. What a horrid man was Rick Beauleigh! Certainly he lacked integrity, or he would not have sent a solicitor to bargain with her in such a manner; and when she chanced to think that a very short time ago she had actually considered succumbing to his attractions, she very much wanted to scream. As it was, she had to force herself to remain seated and reply to Mr. Bagwell in a civil tone. "You must know, Mr. Bagwell, that no sum of money you could advance would ever convince me to leave Seven Hills. And you may tell Mr. Beauleigh that he is wasting his time if he hopes to buy my cooperation in future."

"I thought you might say that." He smiled slightly, and added, "I must admit I should have been disappointed if you had accepted the offer. In fact, I'm rather glad you came dangerously close to marching me out of the house by my ear."

The mental picture he created went a long way toward dispelling Marianna's anger, and she found herself choking back a laugh. "Was I that transparent? Oh, and I was so certain I had covered my anger!"

"Not from me. Never from me, Miss Madison." He was quiet a moment, then slowly, and very gently, he took her hand and said, "I know it would be too much to expect for you to confide in me, but I hope you will tell me, Miss Madison, if ever Mr. Beauleigh causes you the least distress. I can only hope that so far he hasn't stepped beyond the line."

Slightly taken aback, she said quickly, "Oh, not at all, I assure you! He has never done anything—that is, he has never—!" She broke off in deep confusion.

"Never, Miss Madison?" he asked, peering quizzically at her.

"Never. Perhaps Mr. Beauleigh does not find me to his taste."

"With your face and charm? That cannot be," he said gently.

She was just beginning to feel the warm tide of a blush creep up her neck from her collar, when she heard Rick's voice from the door saying, "This is cozy. I can only hope I am intruding."

Marianna quickly snatched her hand from Mr. Bagwell's grasp, a look of abject guilt upon her face. "Mr. Beauleigh! We didn't hear you come in."

"So I gathered," he said, with a pointed glance that sent a fiery blush to Marianna's cheeks.

"You mustn't mind us," said Mr. Bagwell affably. "I was merely assuring Miss Madison that she could count on me to throw a fist at you if ever your behavior becomes intolerable."

Rick's dark brow flew skyward. "Would you, John?"

"Oh, I should try to plant you a facer, to be sure. I doubt very much I should succeed, but by God, I'd try!"

Rick relaxed visibly, and a smile touched his lips. "Did you come out here today just to speak nonsense?"

"Not at all. I have come with some business to discuss with you."

Marianna gratefully seized upon this information as a chance to escape. She rose quickly, saying, "If you must talk of business, you shall not want me about. Please excuse me."

Rick moved slightly to block her path to the door. "There's no need for you to leave, Miss Madison. Stay, won't you?"

"What you and Mr. Bagwell have to say to each other cannot be of interest to me," she said, with a stony look. "I must beg to be excused."

He held the door for her, and no sooner did he close the door upon her, than John Bagwell cast a glinting eye toward him and said, "She's lovely."

"No, she's not," Rick retorted automatically. "Shall I pour you a glass of sherry?"

He crossed the room to a table set with decanters and glasses. From one of the decanters he poured out two glasses and handed one to John.

"Your eyes must be going dim, Rick. Either that or you have noticed how pretty she is and don't care to admit it. I rather think the second explanation is correct, else you wouldn't have been so provoked to see her hand in mine just now."

"You mistake, John. If I was provoked, it was because I noticed a smudge on my coat sleeve as I came in."

"Liar," said Mr. Bagwell good-naturedly. "If you find your Miss Madison attractive, who am I to give you a trimming? She's pretty with a pleasing figure and a mind as bright as a new penny. I'm rather taken with her myself."

"Don't be," recommended Rick. "You and I have been friends too long, and I've seen you take up then discard a score of flirts over the years. I won't have you trifling with Miss Madison."

"You wrong me, Rick!" protested Mr. Bagwell. "My interest in Miss Madison is far from trifling. In fact, I rather think she's quite the most intriguing young woman to enter Newmarket in years. Surely you cannot be so cruel as to warn me off."

"I can be so cruel," said Rick evenly. He took a sip from his glass and considered his friend a moment in thoughtful silence. "Is there any particular reason that compels you to wax rhapsodic over the fair Miss Madison?"

"Not really. But I'd recommend that you enjoy looking at her pretty face while you can, for I very much doubt you will have the opportunity to do so before long."

Rick straightened slightly. "Have you reached a decision, then? Have you determined the true owner of Seven Hills?"

"No, not yet. I'm awaiting the arrival of one more document from London, and then I shall be able to argue the matter one way or the other. But making such a decision may not be necessary, after all. Your lovely Miss Madison may be made to abandon her claim to the property."

"You're chasing rainbows, John. Marianna is the most stubborn female of my acquaintance. She will never be compelled to simply walk away from Seven Hills."

"I think she might. A few moments ago I offered her a modest sum of money if she would but abandon her claim."

"She refused, of course!"

"Of course! But by week's end she might be in a more receptive frame of mind, considering the fact that she is unable to earn a living here, thanks to my efforts."

"Your efforts?" Rick frowned slightly. "What have you done?"

"I merely dropped a few hints here and there about the village. It took very little effort to convince our neighbors that their daughters could do without lessons in French and Italian."

"Who gave you leave to interfere in such a way?"

"You did. You told me you wanted Seven Hills at any cost."

Rick stared at him, an incredulous look upon his face. He dimly recalled having once uttered such words to John Bagwell, but that was long before he had come to know Marianna Madison. Where once he had considered her an adversary, a foe to be vanquished in his quest to possess Seven Hills, he now came to think of her as rather a part of his daily life. And while he still insisted that he would never relinquish Seven Hills willingly, neither did he wish to own the place at the expense of such backdoor methods.

He said darkly, "You know very well it was not my intention to sanction that kind of behavior."

"I know. It's that noble streak of yours. It's always been excessively strong in you—don't bother to deny it!—and I daresay you've missed many an opportunity in life because of it. I, on the other hand, am happily unencumbered by such cursed sensibilities."

It didn't sit well with Rick that his longtime friend was attempting to make light of a situation he considered serious in the extreme. He said dampeningly, "That's between you and your conscience. My conscience, however, tells me that our friendship shall suffer greatly if ever you pull such a dog's trick again. In future, you'll be so good as to leave Miss Madison to me while you concentrate on sorting papers and reading deeds."

"Leave her to you? By all means!" Mr. Bagwell responded, quite unperturbed. He changed the subject then, and they conversed a little while longer, but the mood between them was strained. The more John Bagwell attempted to charm his friend, the more Rick's mood darkened, and when at last John departed, Rick felt almost relieved. He spent some time considering that his friend, in his quest to help, might have caused considerable damage to Rick's relationship with Marianna. He couldn't begin to guess what she might be thinking of him, and if she believed he had sent an envoy to buy her off, she might be very angry, indeed. He could very easily have wrung John Bagwell's neck had he still been at hand, but the satisfaction of doing so would have to wait another day. He was less certain what his action would be when next he found himself alone with Marianna.

Twelve

Rick didn't see Marianna again until dinner. He entered the kitchens to find that the table was set for only two places. Miss Blessington was busily preparing their meal, but turned about when he entered and said, "Those covers are for Master Robin and me, sir. You'll be having your dinner in the dining room."

"Will I?" he asked, in some surprise. "Have I been banished, then?"

"Not at all. It is only that Miss Marianna and I finished cleaning the dining room this afternoon, and it's a sight to behold: all polished and shining and begging to be used. It's about time you and Miss Marianna took your dinner properly, not in the kitchen with an old woman and an imp of a boy."

Rick was quite willing to do as she asked, but Marianna, when she was told of it, blushed hotly.

"Couldn't we just have our dinner in the kitchens as we've been used to?" she asked quickly. "It's so warm and cozy there, and the dining room is much too large for only two people. We shall be lost in such a room."

"Miss Marianna, it's time you started acting the lady of the manor," Miss Blessington replied.

"But who shall serve us?" Marianna demanded.

"I shall."

"Blessing, you—you *can't* do such a thing!"

Her old nurse retorted by saying that she not only could, but would. In the end, Marianna had no choice but to join Rick in the dining room, and when he held her chair for her, then took the seat next to hers at the head of the table, her blushes were so fiery that she might have supposed her face had caught fire. She also discovered that she was suddenly shy in his presence and had to rely upon him to lead the conversation. He did so easily enough, speaking of commonplace topics, asking after Robin and Jemmy, and complimenting Miss Blessington on the delicious meal she had prepared.

Through it all, Marianna answered him politely and did her best to hold her end of the conversation, but try as she might to appear calm and serene, she was vividly and nervously conscious of the fact that they were alone together. Oh, they had been alone before on any number of occasions, but she had never before felt as if her nerves were full of electricity. Her heart was thumping against her ribs to such a degree that she thought he surely must hear it, and her breath was so short, she wondered that she was able to string two sensible words together. She picked at her food, too nervous to swallow more than a few bites, and by the end of their dinner, she was fairly well convinced that she would soon starve to death if she was compelled to take all of her meals tête-è-tête with Rick.

After dinner, he escorted her into the drawing room and ushered her to a chair with a solicitude that she might have found enchanting under any other circumstance. But the recollection of her conversation that afternoon with Mr. Bagwell was still burning brightly in her mind. Difficult, indeed, was it to remember that the pleasant and polite man seated beside her was capable of such treachery as offering up a bribe to get what he wanted. Difficult, too, was it to ignore the manner in which he appeared to be completely at his ease, while she was forced to deal with any number of emotions seething in her breast.

"You don't mind the quiet, do you?" he asked, startling her so that she almost jumped.

"Th—the quiet? What do you mean?"

"I mean that there are any number of people who cannot abide quiet, who think they must fill up any stretch of stillness with words or music or noise. They don't enjoy the peaceful serenity quiet can bring. You, on the other hand, don't seem to mind an evening spent in calm companionship."

"I never thought of it before," she answered simply.

He fell to silence again for a few moments, then said, "I like what you and Miss Blessington have done in this room. It's very pleasant. It's almost as I remember it being when I was a child. There were many nights over the last few years—when I was in Spain with my regiment and later when I was recuperating at Blanfield—that I would think of this room, of its serenity, and long to be in it."

The tone of his voice caused Marianna to look at him curiously. What she detected in his expression kept her silent. In his eyes she saw disappointment, sadness, and loss. It was one of the many mysteries about him that such a self-assured man could speak with such surprising sorrow.

"What is Blanfield, Mr. Beauleigh?" she asked, at last.

"My family seat near Derbyshire. Have you heard of it?"

"No. Is it very large?"

He smiled slightly. "It is, with miles of parkland and a stable that would set your Robin aglow with happiness. Blanfield is large and grand and magnificent in its way, but it's not a home. Not like Seven Hills."

She had a sudden image of Rick in such a setting, the

perfect country gentleman, at ease in the great public rooms and paneled halls of a princely estate. "Why is Blanfield not a home? Weren't your family there?"

"They were, for the most part. I was the youngest of six children, you see, and as I was growing up, my eldest brothers and sisters were leaving Blanfield and going about their lives. They married and set up their own households."

"And eventually you were left alone? That must have been quite wonderful, for you had your parents to yourself, with no siblings demanding that you share their affections."

He tilted his head at her. "So you would think."

The look he cast her caused her heart to tie in knots. He hadn't sounded sorrowful, nor had his tone contained the least trace of self-pity; but she knew instinctively from the look in his eyes that he had long harbored a childhood sadness. Her reaction was to ask him to explain, to beg him to tell her more. She wished to learn what had happened, what had caused that fleeting look in his eyes. Even more, she wanted to make that look go away, and make the smile tug at the corners of his lips as she had seen before.

In the end, she did none of those things. Instead, she gave herself a severe mental scolding and allowed the subject to drop. No probing questions did she ask, nor did she encourage him to confide to her his thoughts; but she was curious over his circumstance and found herself wanting to know more about him and the person he had been.

After a time she left him in the drawing room and retreated to her little blue sitting room on the pretext of working on her poetry. A light rain was falling outside as she sat down at the writing table. She picked up her pen, intent upon her work, but found, instead, that her thoughts dwelt more on Rick than on rhyme. She couldn't concentrate at all on the pages of verse before her and spent a good deal of time thinking pleasant thoughts that centered upon Rick's handsome looks and the pleasing manner in which he had spoken to her at dinner. With very little soul-searching, with hardly any effort at all, Marianna began to wonder if she hadn't fallen a little bit in love with Rick Beauleigh. It was not a stunning revelation, but it was an uncomfortable one.

Rick had warned her once that he would stop at nothing to own Seven Hills, and some devilish imp in the back of her mind caused her to wonder if he hadn't planned to make her love him just so he could beguile her into giving him the property. It was a horrid accusation, one she had no business entertaining, but it persisted. And when she chanced to recall that Mr. Bagwell had spoken of Rick's ruthlessness, she began to wonder if her suspicions might not be well founded.

By the time she prepared for bed, she made the decision to keep her sentiments a secret. Time, she knew, would eventually tell her all she needed to know. Sooner or later she would discover if Rick was merely trying to charm her into giving him what he wanted most. She hoped that was not the case and wished with all her being that his feelings for her had undergone a change similar to her own and that he loved her a little back. Either way, she told herself that she was prepared to accept the outcome and decided that her wisest course of action would be to keep her feelings to herself.

That was a task not easily accomplished, as she learned the next morning. Miss Blessington had dispatched her to the village with a list of errands to accomplish. She was walking along the lane, doing her best to avoid patches of mud from last night's rain, when she looked up and saw a sporting vehicle approaching. She immediately recognized Rick as the driver, and as the carriage drew nearer, she saw that her cousin was seated beside him. Isabelle was peering up at Rick, smiling brightly from beneath the brim of a very fetching bonnet that framed her face perfectly. Rick was concentrating his attention upon the road, and as soon as he spied Marianna, he slowed his horses so he was able to draw up directly beside her.

"Good morning. I wish I had known you were going to the village today. I would have dropped you."

She had always thought he was possessed of a commanding presence, but sitting up in his curricle, with his whip in his hand and his hat set at a rather rakish angle atop his head, she thought it would be impossible to deny him anything. She said, looking up at him from beneath the brim of her bonnet, "Thank you, but I am enjoying the walk."

"Shall you be long in the village? We could wait for you and drive you back to Seven Hills. It would be a tight fit, and we might be uncomfortable for a mile or so, but I daresay we could manage."

Marianna glanced at Isabelle and caught the minatory gleam in her cousin's eyes. She couldn't blame Isabelle, for had Marianna been the one fortunate enough to sit up beside Rick, she, too, would have been loath to share him. "There's no need. Besides, we are going in opposite directions, I believe."

Isabelle bestowed a thin smile upon her. "It's just as well, Mr. Beauleigh. Only look at the mud on her shoes and the dust on the hem of her gown. Why, your beautiful little curricle would be quite ruined were she to climb up into it."

"A little mud doesn't signify," he said impatiently. He held his hand down to her, saying, "Will you ride with us or shall we go on without you?"

"Thank you for the offer, but I shall walk, I think." She stepped back, and Rick gave his horses the office. They set off with a lurch, and Marianna watched Rick and Isabelle drive away. Immediately, she felt a pang of regret, wishing that she were the one who was seated beside Rick instead of her cousin. As she watched, Isabelle said something and laughed, then leaned toward Rick just enough so her shoulder brushed against his. His arm slipped briefly about Isabelle's slim shoulders, and he gave them a rather proprietary squeeze.

Marianna turned quickly around and began to walk toward the village, trying mightily to rid her mind of the picture of them together, but it did no good. The image haunted her as she executed Miss Blessington's commissions and teased her still as she returned home in time for her to join Rick in the blue sitting room for his customary French lesson. The lesson didn't last long. Rick was preoccupied and made no attempt to hide the fact that he was having a difficult time concentrating on the business at hand. Marianna tried to be patient and painstakingly repeated herself when necessary. She was half-tempted to reach across and touch his hand, and beg that he pay attention to her, but she didn't.

Instead, she quietly closed her book, and said softly, "You haven't paid the least heed to anything I've said." When he didn't answer, she studied him a moment, debating the wisdom of issuing a thorough scold. In the end, she decided to see if she could cajole him out of his present dark humor, and said, in a markedly lowered voice, "Nonsense, Miss Madison! I've listened to every word you've spoken in your perfect French accent, and it is my dearest dream to someday be as proficient at speaking the language as you!"

He looked at her then, a wry little smile tugging at his lips. "I've been a little rude, haven't I?"

"No," she said pleasantly, "you've been *very* rude. What were you thinking of, I wonder, that would make you so forgetful of your surroundings."

"I was thinking of your cousin," he said. "Tell me, what do you know of her? Would you say she is a sentimental woman?"

She rather thought that Rick could not have raised a more distasteful subject. Discussing Isabelle Madison, hearing Rick extol her many charms, was not a possibility Marianna cared to entertain. She said rigidly, "I'm afraid I am not well acquainted with my cousin."

His brows went up. "I'm not asking you to reveal family secrets, Marianna. I'm simply asking what sort of person you judge her to be."

"You would be better equipped to answer that question, Mr. Beauleigh, for *you* spend a great deal more time with her than I." She had meant to sound dispassionate, but suffered the odd notion that she had sounded snippy instead. Impatient with her own conduct, she then proceeded to make matters worse by saying, "I cannot advise you where my cousin is concerned. The fact that you prefer each other's company—"

"Prefer each other's company!" he interrupted explosively. "Where did you get a notion like that?"

"You cannot deny that you spend a great deal of time with her."

"I spend more time with my horses, and I fancy I spend rather a bit more time with you, if the truth were to be told. What's got into you today?" he asked, frowning at her. "You're never so prickly!"

It was beyond her ability to admit that the devilish imp of jealousy was riding upon her shoulders, and she said, rather sullenly, "I'm not prickly at all. I simply do not understand why you would wish to remind me that you are on better terms with my relatives than I. *You* may share my uncle's dinner and take my cousin driving. *I* may not have the pleasure of doing either of those things."

His frown increased as he stared thoughtfully at her. "Marianna . . ." He stopped, not at all certain what to say next. An apology hovered on his lips, but he wasn't entirely convinced he had done anything to warrant begging her forgiveness. Still, he could tell she was upset and deeply agitated; she could not bring herself to look at him, and he had heard the hurt in her voice. Impulsively, he said, "Marianna, drive out with me."

She looked at him quickly. "What did you say?"

"Come with me to the stables. We'll put Pepperpot to the gig and drive out into the countryside, just to find some peace together. We'll talk about things—about the weather, books, politics—anything you want. We'll simply get to know each other a little better." He paused, watching her, frowning a little as he tried to gauge her response. "Marianna, please drive out with me."

Marianna could barely force herself to consider his words. Her mind was filled with the memory of Rick and Isabelle Madison in just such a scene as he had described, driving together in the close confines of his curricle, his broad shoulders brushing hers, their heads drawn close together as they laughed over some shared secret.

"Marianna," he said, with a rather bewildered laugh, "are you even listening to me?"

"Yes," she answered quietly, as she tried to shake that hateful image from her mind.

"Then, come with me." He took a step toward her and was surprised to see her stiffen slightly. "Must I ask your Miss Blessington to come along as gooseberry? I shall do so, if it will convince you to accept."

"No," she said, with a determined shake of her head. "I can't go with you."

"And may I ask why not?"

She didn't quite know how to answer him. She would rather die than confess that she couldn't bear to share as second choice the same pleasures her cousin Isabelle had already known. Nor could she tell him that she couldn't possibly be with him, enjoying his company, knowing all the while that she was with him only because Isabelle couldn't be.

He said, rather bitterly, "You've no scruples when it comes to driving with John Bagwell, I notice."

"John Bagwell?" she repeated with some surprise. "But he has nothing to say to the matter!"

"Doesn't he? You've thrown his virtues in my face countless times before," retorted Rick, with a healthy dose of exaggeration, "and you've never tried to conceal the fact that you prefer his company to mine."

"No! It's not like that at all," she said earnestly, wondering how a simple invitation to drive in the country could have careened down such a path.

"Isn't it? Then, tell me, Marianna, what *is* it like?"

She trembled on the brink of uttering what was truly in her heart, but stopped herself in time, knowing that the merest hint of her true feelings would result in the unthinkable happening. As much as she had fought against it, she had already admitted to herself that she was a little bit in love with him. To admit such a thing to Rick, to even allow him a glimpse of her feelings, would prove a mortifying prospect. It was far better, she judged, to let him think she was indifferent to him, than to betray her true feelings.

She said, in a low voice, "Please don't ask me to explain, but believe me when I tell you I cannot accept your invitation." She stopped, realizing how ridiculously prim she had sounded. She cast him a rather pleading look, as if she might be able to make him understand through sheer will.

He didn't understand. In fact, he was having a devil of a time understanding anything about her. How she could be an enjoyable companion one day and a bristling adversary the next, he had no idea. In the past few days he had begun to see her soften a bit where he was concerned, and though he judged that some of her change of heart may have been prompted by sympathy to his condition, he had begun to realize that she was not quite so defensive with him. He had begun to believe, too, that she had come to view him in a different, more favorable light. On this day, however, there was no softness in her gray eyes when she looked at him, and no timid glances his direction when she thought he wasn't aware. In truth, he was at a loss to understand her, and said, rather resignedly, "I hope someday you'll explain to me what I have done to earn such treatment."

He didn't press her further, but took his leave. Leaning back in the chair at her desk, Marianna felt instantly and utterly alone. If only she had the last five minutes to live over again, how different they would be! In the end, she comforted herself with the notion that she had done the right thing in rebuffing Rick. Only by keeping a safe distance between them would she ensure he would remain unaware of what was in her heart. In the quiet emptiness of her sitting room, those reassurances sounded unconvincing even to her own ears.

Thirteen

There was no great decision to be made concerning Marianna's attire for the party at Madison House. Her white satin ball dress with its lace bodice and embroidered hem was her best gown, and she had received enough compliments in the past when wearing it to know she looked well in it. The white fabric complemented her skin very well, and set off to dramatic effect her dark hair, bright eyes and rosy lips. She wore no ornamentation except a short strand of pearls about her neck, a gauze scarf that she linked carefully about her arms, and a pearl-studded comb, which Miss Blessington affixed among the black curls arranged atop her head.

When at last her toilet was complete, Miss Blessington opened the door to admit Robin and Jemmy. Jemmy shyly hovered near the door, saying nothing, but noting everything about her appearance with his wide, intelligent eyes. Robin circled his sister, and said approvingly, "By Jove, you're looking bang up to the knocker, Marianna!"

She stifled a gasp and demanded, "Robin Madison, where on earth did you learn such a horrid phrase?"

"I—nowhere," he said, having caught the ominous tone in her voice.

Simply because he wouldn't admit to the source of his language didn't at all mean that she couldn't guess. "The stables, I should think. Robin, dear, you mustn't repeat everything you hear Currant say."

"Oh, it wasn't Currant; it was Mr. Beauleigh. I told him that Orion was quite the prettiest thing I'd ever seen, and he said he rather thought the same of you whenever you wear your blue dress."

Marianna felt herself blush to the roots of her hair. For the briefest of moments she tottered between the high road of begging her brother not repeat everything he heard, and begging to be told more. So, Rick Beauleigh was not quite so unfeeling as he would have her believe! For the first time since making his acquaintance, she was filled with a little hope.

Miss Blessington handed her the pair of gloves she would wear that night. "You look very pretty, indeed, miss, and your dear mother would be bursting with pride to see you so if she were here."

"Do you think so?" she asked. "To tell you the truth, I do feel pretty, and the pearls in my hair are quite the nicest touch. Thank you, dear Blessing," she said, and planted a light kiss upon her old nurse's cheek.

"Nonsense!" said Miss Blessington gruffly. "The way you carry on, you'd think they were diamonds! Now, mind you don't tread upon your skirts and watch where you step until you are safely in the house so your slippers shall be clean."

"I will, Blessing. Oh, how I wish you were going with me. I shall be nervous without you."

"Old women are not invited to fashionable parties," said Miss Blessington simply. "Besides, you'll have Mr. Beauleigh to look after you and squire you about."

Marianna drew a deep breath and took one last glimpse of herself in the glass. She knew she was looking her best, and that knowledge went a long way toward taking away some of the nervousness she felt as she made her way down to the drawing room. She was to meet Rick here, and together they were to ride to Madison House. Currant had promised to wear livery for the occasion and transport them in regal style.

She entered the room to find Rick there before her, standing at the hearth, staring into the flames of a brightly burning fire. He didn't notice her at first, and she paused just inside the door, watching him. She had never seen him looking so handsome. His dark evening coat was expensively tailored, and his cravat lay against his neck like an immaculate fall of fresh snow. His hair was brushed into a fashionable style and glowed beneath the candlelight of the room. So exactly were his coat and breeches fitted to his figure that they appeared to be molded about him, and she had a clear impression of his solid strength.

He looked up presently and saw her. He straightened away from the mantel, a slight smile crooked the corner of his mouth, and a gleam of appreciation lit his blue eyes as his gaze swept over her. "Marianna! I didn't hear you just now. Come in!" With a slight wave of his hand, he drew her toward the fire. "I'm convinced you'll be much more comfortable near the hearth, for the room is chilled, and we cannot have you arrive at Madison House covered in gooseflesh."

This remark, while delivered in a softly tantalizing voice, was not at all the loverlike speech of her dreams; but then she realized that his eyes had not once strayed from her since she entered the room, and her heart felt a little lighter.

"You look very pretty tonight, Marianna," he murmured.

Had she obeyed her impulse, she would have blurted in return that *he* looked even more handsome than usual. It was a difficult task to control her emotions and merely thank him in a quiet, dignified tone, but she managed to do so.

She held her hands out toward the fire, unsure what to say, knowing she couldn't look at him for fear her expression might betray her feelings for him. Knowing she was in love with a man who didn't love her in return left her feeling understandably reticent and disturbingly vulnerable.

"Tonight is not the night for you to be shy, Marianna," said Rick, with a touch of gentle amusement in his voice. "I am relying on you to enjoy yourself."

"And what of you? Will you not enjoy yourself?" she asked.

"My greatest entertainment is in seeing you as you are right now, with your lips smiling in anticipation and your eyes glowing with the light of a hundred chandeliers."

Her gray eyes flew to meet his gaze. If only his slight smile were not quite so charming, she wouldn't now be wrestling with the knowledge she was in love with him! If only she could place her trust in him, instead of having to recall that since the day of their acquaintance he had set himself up as her nemesis. If only she could read past the light of appreciation in his blue eyes as they rested upon her. Only then might she be certain that he was speaking sincerely and not merely flirting with her. Though there had been a note of sincerity in his voice, she could not allow herself to trust it. She smiled up at him and said, very politely, "That is the nicest compliment I have ever received, sir."

"You deserve more, you know, but I don't think you are of a mind right now to hear them. Shall we be on our way, instead?"

In the hall he waited patiently as she drew on her long gloves and Miss Blessington set her cape about her shoulders with as much care as she might have set a pane of glass upon the tip of a pin. Marianna gave her a light kiss good night and begged her not to wait up for her. Then she placed a nervous hand upon Rick's arm, and they set off down the stairs and into the waiting carriage.

Madison House appeared a much more inviting residence on this evening than it had been when first Marianna had visited. The front of the house was ablaze with lights shining from every room. No sooner did they lay off their things, than they were escorted up the stairs and through a number of galleries to the main drawing room. There the dinner guests were assembled, and Marianna recognized many of the faces who turned to look when her name was announced with Rick's.

Isabelle came forward in a swath of green silk over which she wore a robe of embroidered lace. The diamond drops at her ears were quite large, but tasteful, and caught the light of the candles with her every move.

She came toward them, a smile on her lips, saying, "There you are! I was beginning to believe some accident had befallen you. Come and greet my uncle, and then I shall make you known to a handful of our more worthy guests!"

Since she made this remark well within earshot of those who were not fortunate enough to fall within this category, a good number of nearby guests fell to silence and critically eyed Marianna and Rick. Marianna felt herself flush rosily, but she managed to execute a creditable curtsy when she at last found herself standing before her uncle.

Cecil Madison was a much older gentleman than Marianna had thought. He was small and sickly-looking with a pale, gray face upon which he had affixed for the occasion two patches: one at his chin and the second on his cheek just below his left eye. Also for the occasion—and to Isabelle's utter mortification—he had donned an old-fashioned powdered and curled wig, dressed in long tendrils that were intended to fall down his back from where they had been gathered at the base of the wig by a bow of black grossgrain. That, he had informed Isabelle earlier, was the manner in which a true gentleman dressed before it became the fashion for men of breeding to dress like stableboys. But since making his entrance on the arm of his niece, Cecil Madison's wig had gone decidedly askew, and the patch on his cheek, under the bright lights of the drawing room, only accentuated his pallor.

Marianna was deeply disappointed. In her estimation, he didn't at all behave as an uncle should. She had known he wasn't at all disposed toward strong family ties, but she had always hoped that when at last she met him, he would welcome her to the family or, at the very least, recognize some obligation where she was concerned. Instead, she suffered the distinct impression that he hadn't the faintest idea who she was, and when she ventured to remark how well he was looking, he retorted in a quarrelsome tone, "I haven't been well for years and wouldn't be here now if I hadn't been dragged from my bed. I daresay I could very well fall over this moment and not a one of these villains would notice!"

"He enjoys perfect health," said Isabelle firmly. "You mustn't pay him the least heed when he speaks so. Now, Uncle, you remember Mr. Beauleigh, don't you?"

Rick executed a slight bow, to which Cecil Madison responded by saying, rather acidly, "Back to avail yourself of more of my hospitality, are you?"

"And of your engaging conversation, sir," said Rick, quite solemnly.

Marianna braced herself against the storm she knew must follow such impudent words, but Cecil Madison simply eyed Rick with his usual expression of rancor and grunted.

Isabelle then proceeded to fulfill her promise to introduce them to other guests that were worthy of their notice. They paraded in front of Marianna and Rick in a sea of faces and names, until Marianna was very much afraid she had forgotten half of the people she had met. She was saved the effort of trying to commit to memory even more names when dinner was announced. The assembled gentlemen and ladies began pairing off by order of consequence to go in to dinner. Isabelle, with her full lips pressed into a determined line, laced her hand through Rick's arm in a rather proprietary pose and ignored any other, more consequential claim to her hand.

It was a bold thing to do, and more than one guest observed it, including Marianna, who knew the acute discomfort of having to wait for a gentleman to appear and claim the privilege of escorting her into the dining room. She was not compelled to wait long, but in those few awkward moments, she chanced a look at Rick, only to find his eyes upon her, his brow frowning in slight concern. She would have preferred it if he had shaken Isabelle's hold from his arm and insisted that he and he alone would escort her into dinner. But he did neither of those things. The fact that it would have been scarcely civil of him to abandon Isabelle was a thought that crossed her mind. But she dismissed it, for he was being civil to Isabelle at *her* expense, and that irrational twinge of jealousy left her wishing he were less of a gentleman where Isabelle was concerned.

Her partner was Mr. Larimer, a gentleman to whom she had been introduced some minutes before, and he performed his part very creditably. His conversation at dinner was light and his intellect was dim, but he managed to keep her entertained throughout the meal. Once or twice, when Mr. Larimer's attention was captured by the lady on his other side, Marianna glanced down the table and was pleased to see Mr. Bagwell in attendance. His eyes met hers. He smiled slightly, and she felt immediately comforted. At the opposite end of the table Rick and Isabelle were seated together. Rick was speaking quietly, and Isabelle was looking up at him in rapt attention, her meal forgotten as she hung on every word that issued from his lips. It was apparent, she was sure, to anyone who saw them so, that Isabelle was very much enamored of Rick Beauleigh. It was also certain that she was not above making her interest known.

At the end of the meal, the ladies retired but waited only a short time before the gentlemen joined them. Marianna was engaged in trifling conversation with a matron who was recounting the recent affliction of her four children with a horrid influenza, when she saw the door open and Rick enter the room. Isabelle saw him, too, but since she was also engaged and was herself in the middle of relaying an amusing story, she was unable to break off and beg him to join her. Very casually, but purposefully, too, he traversed the room, exchanging greetings with those of the guests with whom he was acquainted. In a very little while he was with Marianna and stood a little behind her, his hand on the back of her chair. He didn't interrupt her conversation, but she felt a surge of excitement which was entirely due to his nearness.

In very short order the rest of the guests began to arrive. Rick offered her his arm, and together they moved with the others toward the long gallery. Two liveried footmen threw open the doors to that room, signaling the musicians to strike up the chords of a simple quadrille.

Marianna's interest quickened. "Oh, is there to be dancing? How wonderful!" she exclaimed, feeling herself come alive.

"I have the oddest notion you have never before attended an assembly such as this," he said, watching her with interest. "You may correct me if I am wrong, Miss Madison."

"It is true, I'm afraid. I'm woefully without experience in these matters and regretfully admit that this shall be my first party. You mustn't smile at me so," she said, scolding him slightly, "for I am speaking nothing but the truth. In the past, I was much too young for such an assembly, and by the time I finally reached an age when I might go to one or two of the entertainments in the village where I grew up, I was dressed in mourning. Happily, no such barriers exist anymore, and I may look forward to a perfect evening," she said, feeling a little dazzled by the prospect of spending the next few hours amid the bright lights and the music.

After a few moments she became aware that he was quiet beside her and looked up to find that he was watching her, his brows a little raised, and his expression unreadable.

She suffered the odd notion that she had revealed too much, that she never should have admitted to her lack of social experience, certainly not with Isabelle in the same room and ready to clutch him by the sleeve and claim him as her own. For once in her life she wished she had descended from the more sophisticated branch of the Madison family. "I suppose you think I'm rather foolish," she said.

"Not at all," he answered. "I think you're lovely."

He could not have uttered any other words that would have had a greater effect upon her. She had always thought him handsome and a splendid figure of a man, and she had known, too, that her attraction for him had steadily increased since the moment of their meeting. Still, she had always been able to maintain a sensible pose where he was concerned. But with those four simple words, Marianna was instantly reduced to the rank of a stupidly romantic schoolgirl. Very easily might she have spent the remainder of the evening staring up at him with admiring eyes while she mentally catalogued his many heroic qualities, had not her more practical side come to the fore. She blushed and stammered a thank-you, and turned her attention upon the dancers, but her thoughts remained with Rick.

A gentleman led Isabelle out into the center of the room, and another couple followed. Before long the squares were formed and the music began. Marianna watched the dancers, her eyes alight, her spirits soaring. How much she wished she were among them, moving gracefully to the steps of the music, with Rick as her partner.

But that was a wish that did not bear fruit. Rick did not ask her to dance, but merely stood by her side in companionable silence. And when the dance ended and the next set was formed, she felt the beginnings of a keen sense of disappointment.

"May I have this dance, Miss Madison?"

Marianna looked up quickly to find Mr. Bagwell at her side, smiling kindly.

Her first impulse was to demure, for she still held fast to the hope that she might share her first dance with Rick, but the music was too alluring to be denied. She placed her hand on Mr. Bagwell's and joined the other dancers.

Mr. Bagwell performed his part credibly and made an excellent partner, and when their dance was done, he led Marianna back to Rick's side.

He bowed over her hand and thanked her prettily for the dance, then cast a sidelong look at Rick. "Miss Madison is a delightful dancer—you're missing out on a great treat, you know, Beauleigh."

"I've consigned myself to that fact," he answered evenly.

"For once I can claim that dotty leg of yours to my advantage. Usually you're the one who beguiles the ladies with sympathy," Mr. Bagwell said, with a laugh.

To Marianna's thinking, his was a curious observation. She could not recall a time when Rick had ever elicited sympathy for his injury. Instead, she rather thought he made a great effort to disguise the extent of the trouble it caused him.

Mr. Bagwell left them after only a few more words of conversation, and Marianna found herself wondering a little about Rick. She had been thinking that her enjoyment of the evening would be complete only if he danced with her, and she had felt a little sorry that he had not made any such offer; but that was before Mr. Bagwell's words had reminded her that Rick's injured leg prevented his doing anything more strenuous than slowly walking the perimeter of the room.

She tried to gauge his expression, to determine for herself if he was sorry for his situation or longed to behave as the other gentlemen did and join in the dancing, but she could determine nothing in his countenance but warmth and unconcealed interest whenever his eyes alighted upon her.

She reveled in his attentions and contrived to keep him amused with bits of observations about the party and the other guests in attendance. Her conversation was interrupted by a gentleman who asked her to dance, an offer which she declined. She demurred, too, the next offer for her hand.

"Have you lost your taste for dancing so soon, Marianna?" Rick asked.

She tried to make her voice sound languid. "Not precisely, but it does appear to me that one country dance is very much like another, you see."

"Or perhaps your heart is a little more tender than you care to admit." She was about to protest, but he cut her off, saying in a gentle voice, "You shall not betray me if you dance, Marianna. If you enjoy yourself, I shall not complain—as long as I may have your promise that you shall return to my side after each set."

That was a promise she did not hesitate to make, for she could think of nothing more wonderful than to know that Rick wished her companionship.

Thereafter, she danced every dance, and knew the deep satisfaction of being a popular and sought-after dance partner. After each set, she dutifully returned to Rick's side, and felt the exquisite happiness of knowing that the most dashing man of her acquaintance wished to be with her. It was a heady feeling, and she reveled in it. No force on earth, she thought, could intrude upon the enchantment of this evening. For the first time since making the acquaintance of her cousin, Marianna was able to smile at Isabelle with genuine happiness.

Isabelle joined them with a smile of sweetness upon her lips. "I had no notion, cousin, that you were such an accomplished dancer and such a sought-after partner, too! Mr. Beauleigh, I think my little cousin has earned the attention of at least one of our neighborhood's reigning bachelors. I know one gentleman in particular means to ask her for a second dance."

"I shall decline, of course," said Marianna quickly. "In fact, I was rather thinking I shall sit out the next few dances, for the assembly has become a trifle close."

Rick looked at her with a slight frown. "This room is overwarm. I'll bring you a cool drink, Marianna."

When he had gone, Isabelle flicked a look of disdain

over Marianna. "He's very solicitous. How long has he been so?"

"I cannot think what you mean," replied Marianna, feeling unnaturally defensive. "Mr. Beauleigh has always been kind to me and my family."

"That's not what you were saying a mere week ago. In fact, I seem to recall when I delivered to you the invitations for this evening that you were still insisting that he must be put from Seven Hills."

"Nothing has changed in that regard, cousin. I still wish him to leave and allow my family and me to live quietly, as we had planned. But I must admit that we— Mr. Beauleigh and I—have come to an understanding of sorts. We know each other a little better, I think."

"How much better?" demanded Isabelle, with glittering eyes.

"Not well, for Mr. Beauleigh never speaks of himself or his life. I can only tell you that we are more companionable now, and he has been kind to me and my brother. Why, he has even charmed our Miss Blessington, and that was not an easy task."

"I cannot imagine a Beauleigh seeking to charm any servant," Isabelle said, with a brittle laugh.

"You have seen our living situation, cousin," Marianna reminded her, "and you have seen for yourself the lack of servants at Seven Hills. There is only my old nurse and Currant on the rolls, and the work is often too much for them. Mr. Beauleigh is not above helping. Why, once, when I was cleaning the draperies in the drawing room, he—" She stopped short, as she recalled with a flood of memory the manner in which Rick had plucked her from the chair and held her in his arms for one brief but exquisite moment.

Thankfully, Isabelle either failed to notice Marianna's blushes or mistook them for a sign of some other emotion, for she demanded, "How can you be so foolish? Rick Beauleigh cleaning draperies? Next you shall tell me he cleans stable stalls. Honestly, cousin, don't you know who he is?"

"Of course I know. He's Rick Beauleigh and—" She caught the look of utter incredulity in Isabelle's eye and said, rather wearily, "If you're talking about his being a hero in the war, I know about that, too."

"My God, you're stupid," said Isabelle, with disgust. "How can you claim to be a Madison and yet know so little of the world?"

"What are you talking about?"

"I'm talking about Rick Beauleigh—the man with whom you have shared a house for the better part of the last month. Doesn't the name Beauleigh mean anything to you?"

Marianna recognized that question as the very same question Rick had asked her the night of their meeting when first he had told her his name. Just as on that evening, the name meant nothing to her, and so she told Isabelle.

"Then, let me enlighten you, cousin. Mr. Beauleigh is the youngest son of an earl. His grandmother is the daughter of a duchess. The Beauleighs are among the first one hundred families in all of England. Their wealth is boundless, and they dine with kings and princes. And you—! You set him to cleaning draperies!"

"But he never mentioned to me any of this! How could I know?"

"Hasn't he ever spoken of his family? Hasn't he ever described to you the rich history of the Beauleigh name?"

"I know nothing of Mr. Beauleigh except that he served on the Peninsula and was wounded. Sometimes when he becomes bored with his French lessons, he tries to engage me in conversation, but he speaks not at all of his family."

Isabelle's green eyes widened. "French lessons? What French lessons?"

"Every afternoon I instruct Mr. Beauleigh in speaking French."

"You're giving Ulrick Beauleigh French lessons?" Isabelle repeated incredulously. "Are you mad?"

"Not at all. Don't you think he is intelligent enough to learn French?" Marianna demanded, ready to fly to Rick's defense. "I assure you, he is an apt pupil."

"You little fool, he's a Beauleigh! Why, his very name is French!"

Marianna stood staring at her, teetering between bewilderment and dawning realization. "But he said . . . he wished he had known another language when he was with his regiment."

"Portuguese, maybe, or the language of some wretched little country halfway across the world, perhaps. I assure you, Rick Beauleigh speaks fluent French, as well as Spanish and Italian. His father saw to that before he went on the Grand Tour. Honestly, cousin, haven't you any sense?"

Apparently not. At least, that's what she was beginning to realize as the meaning of Isabelle's words began to slowly penetrate her chaotic thoughts. So, Rick had tricked her into believing that he spoke no second language! She cudgeled her mind, trying to think of some explanation for his behavior, but in the end she could only imagine that he had participated in the charade of French lessons only to hoax her. He had spent time with her, flattered her, played against her vanity—all so he might beguile her into bending to his will. How easily had she danced to his tune! He must have gauged her experience very well and known that she had never been in love before, never even engaged in a mere flirtation. He, on the other hand, must be a man of vast experience, she now judged, for he had known the exact look to give her, the very words to say to her that could be counted upon to leave her a little bemused, a little breathless, and very much wanting more. She didn't know which caused her the greater shame: the fact that she had been duped by a handsome man or the fact that she still didn't wish to believe him capable of such treachery.

But treachery it had been, and she was now convinced that he had been speaking nothing but the truth when he warned her he would have Seven Hills at any cost. How foolish she had been to give her heart to him, when her brain had warned her time and again that he was not to be trusted.

How she was to face him again—what she was to say to him—she could hardly think. Should she demand from him an explanation? Should she denounce his behavior before the prying eyes of their assembled neighbors? Or should she force herself to behave as if nothing had happened and dance and laugh as though her heart were not broken? She knew herself unable to maintain such a charade. Rick Beauleigh might be well-versed in deception, but Marianna Madison was not. She could not face him.

She uttered a disjointed excuse to Isabelle and set off across the room, anxious to reach the door, the carriage, and Seven Hills before Rick even realized she was gone.

In a very short while, Marianna had claimed her cloak and made her way down to the front hall. The Madisons' very proper butler called for her carriage and advised her, in a tone more regal than solicitous, that the weather had changed.

It had changed, indeed. While Marianna had been

dancing the night away, reveling in the knowledge that Rick had sought her company above all others, a rainstorm had blown in on a northern wind. She pulled the hood of her cloak up over her head and stepped across the threshold into the night. She was immediately pelted by wind and rain and moved quickly toward the carriage. Currant was there, holding the door, and offered her a hand up, asking, "And is Mr. Beauleigh behind you, miss? I shouldn't wish to keep you or the horses standing in this weather."

Feeling as though a great weight were pressing against her chest, Marianna said miserably, "I am going on without Mr. Beauleigh. Please, Currant, do not let us wait any longer."

Currant cast her a quick look, but he was too well trained to betray curiosity before her. He asked her no questions but spread a soft rug over her legs and shut the door. The carriage gave a slight lurch as he climbed up onto the box, and a moment later the vehicle moved forward.

The short drive to Seven Hills might very well have been one of the longest journeys Marianna ever had to endure. Over and over again did she replay in her mind the persuasiveness of Rick's words, the charm of his smile. How effective had they been! And when she chanced to recall how easily she had succumbed to his allure, she could have screamed aloud.

So, Rick Beauleigh was a man of wealth and noble birth, and yet he had contrived to hide those facts and present himself as nothing more than a veteran of the war. She guessed he had done so to disguise the fact that his pockets were deep, but that won him no favor in her eyes. If he were truly wealthy, he could have any home in England as his own, but he chose, instead, to center his attention on Seven Hills. He chose, instead, to fight her for the only place she could call home. Whether he did so out of spite or malice, she could not guess; she knew only that he had contrived to needlessly turn her world upside down.

That act alone she might have forgiven, and she might have excused his duplicity. But he had contrived to make her fall in love with him, knowing full well that he did so merely to gain an advantage over her. That she could not forgive.

When the carriage pulled up at the front door of Seven Hills, she was able to maintain a tenuous hold over her storming emotions. Currant threw open the carriage door, but before he let down the steps, he said, "Miss Madison, while I was driving I was thinking, and I hope you'll answer me truthfully when I say I don't believe Mr. Beauleigh knows where you are right now, does he?"

"If you're asking whether I took my leave of Mr. Beauleigh before leaving Madison House, I did not. But there is no cause for alarm, for I am home and none the worse for traveling less than two miles without an escort."

"Yes, miss, but I don't think Mr. Beauleigh will like it, once he hears of it," said Currant pessimistically.

"I, for one, shall not tell him." In fact, she had every intention of never speaking another word to that horrid man for the balance of her natural life.

Currant helped her down and would have escorted her into the darkened house had she allowed it, but she waved him away, insisting that he return to Madison House to await his master's pleasure.

In truth, she could not bear another moment of conversation and having to pretend that nothing was amiss. She wished for little more than to find a place of calm and quiet where she might be by herself. Her wish was granted; she entered the house to find it dark and silent.

Upstairs, she found Robin and Jemmy in bed, and when she quietly opened the door to the chamber she shared with Miss Blessington, she found that good lady abed as well, propped against a wall of pillows, a candle still burning low on the bedside table, an open book upon her lap.

From habit, Marianna retreated to the one place she could rely upon to provide some measure of solace. As soon as she entered the little blue sitting room, she felt some small sense of comfort. She discarded her cape and gloves and struck the fire in the hearth. As the first flames glowed, then sprang to life, Marianna held her cold hands out to be warmed, knowing full well that no simple hearth fire would ever be able to warm away the pervasive chill that surrounded her heart.

The heat from the flames intensified, warming her hands and legs and drying the hem of her skirt where her cloak had allowed the rain to soak the fabric. She turned around, intent upon drying the back of her gown and chasing away the remaining chill. That was when she saw it. The stain on the papered wall. A stain of dampness that spread insidiously down from the ceiling line on the far side of the room. She knew in an instant what had happened; the haphazard repairs of oiled cloth and stones had shifted or come undone in the weather, and now the rain was invading her home, her sitting room. Her haven.

As Marianna stood staring at the intrusive blotch on the wall, all the feelings she had entertained on the drive home—the melancholy, the overwhelming hurt—departed. They were gone in an instant, replaced by anger. Anger that was directed solely at Rick. In that moment she could not have been more furious: furious that he had ever come into her life, furious that he should defy her at every turn, furious that he would stoop so low as to make love to Isabelle Madison merely to gain an advantage and steal Seven Hills away.

He had contributed nothing to the upkeep of the place, she realized, as her temper mounted. Oh, he had once helped push the furniture about the drawing room, and he had seen to the cleaning of the stables so his horses might live in comfort; but when the subject turned to maintaining any other aspect of Seven Hills, Rick Beauleigh had firmly refused to help her.

As she watched the gray stain deepen over the papered wall, Marianna's anger reached its pinnacle. Very well! She didn't need his help! she told herself defiantly. She would fix the roof herself, and no sooner did she come to that decision, than she impetuously pulled her wet cape back about her shoulders. She tied the ribbons securely at her throat and thrust open the window sash with an unnecessary force.

In the comparative dryness of her cozy sitting room, fixing the roof seemed like such a simple task. She had only to climb out the window, as she had seen Mr. Hendrick do, and inch her way no more than a few feet up the valley of the dormer and securely draw the oiled cloth back over the missing roof tiles. But no sooner did she open the window, than the wind-driven rain began to pelt her.

Almost she lost her resolve, but anger and pride drove her on. Resolutely, she stepped up on the sill, out into the storm. Her cloak whipped wildly in the wind, tugging at the ribbons that secured it to her throat, denying her arms and skirts the merest protection from the rain. Within minutes her gown was soaked through, and she could feel little rivulets of rainwater running down her legs and arms.

For a moment she was half-tempted to turn back, to retreat to the warmth and dryness of the little blue sitting room, but that temptation was quickly vanquished. She would show Rick Beauleigh that she didn't need his help. She would prove to him that she could take much better care of Seven Hills than he.

Mulishly she fought to control the swirling cloak and searched for a foothold in the roof. Slowly, cautiously, she began to inch her way up the dormer.

The roof tiles were slick beneath her—for every two feet she climbed, she could have sworn she slid back one—but she soldiered on, clutching at the roof with cold fingers, inching her way up the pitch of the dormer to where the oiled cloth danced maniacally in the wind.

Holding on as best she could with one hand, Marianna batted at the cloth with the other and managed to draw it back over the area where the roof tiles were missing. Only then did she understand the true nature of her situation; only then did she realize she couldn't patch the leaking roof alone. She had, after all, but two hands: one for holding down the wind-whipped cloth, and one for clutching desperately at the roof tiles to keep from slipping down the angle of the dormer and over the edge. How, then, was she going to move any of the anchoring stones back over the cloth?

She nudged one of the errant stones with her elbow, but instead of rolling it over the cloth as she intended, she merely sent it skipping down the tiles. She made a move to grab at it, but she was no match for the pitch of the roof. The stone tripped merrily away from her, down the roofline and over the edge, to land with a sickening thud onto the rain-soaked ground below.

Too late did she realize her mistake, for her lunge for the stone had played havoc with the hold she had established. Slowly, terrifyingly, she began to slip facedown along the tiles. She clawed at the roof, but her fingers were too wet and cold to function. Her feet, still clad in soft dancing slippers, found no foothold in the rain-soaked tiles.

She was going to fall. Just as surely as that stone had tumbled from the roof but moments before, Marianna knew she was going to slide over the edge of the dormer and fall to the sodden ground below. There was nothing to stop her slow, inexorable slide, and there was nothing on the ground below to break her fall. Crazily, she wondered if the fall would kill her, and then, just as she felt certain her feet were about to clear the eave and dangle in space, she felt an unaccustomed pressure about her ankle.

Someone had hold of her leg and, with a grip like iron, began to drag her sideways toward the open window.

Fourteen

If he lived to be one hundred, thought Rick Beauleigh, he would never understand the workings of the female mind. What might have possessed Marianna to leave the assembly without so much as a word of explanation, he could not guess. He knew only that he had been angered to find her gone, and a little disappointed, too. She had spent the better part of the evening at his side, smiling at him, charming him, looking more lovely than any other woman in the room. For a few hours, while the music played and the lights burned brightly in the gallery, there had existed no conflict between them; not once had either of them mentioned Seven Hills or money or any other of the various frictions that existed between them in the past. They had been but a man and a woman, together enjoying an evening's entertainment with neighbors and friends.

What might have occurred to send her rushing back to Seven Hills without a word of explanation, he could not guess, although he rather suspected Isabelle Madison had something to do with it. By the time he was able to politely make his excuses to Isabelle and make some discreet inquiries after Marianna, she had already gone, and he had spent some impatient minutes waiting for Currant to return with the carriage.

Now, as he traveled the short distance from Madison House to Seven Hills, he realized he was more curious over Marianna's behavior than he was angry; but that sentiment changed rapidly as soon as the carriage bowled up the drive and swung about at the front of the house.

Currant brought the horses to a stop and let out an involuntary, "Good God! Sir, look!"

Rick threw open the carriage door. The house was dark except for a light that shone through one of the dormered windows on the uppermost floor. And just above that window, he could see a dark silhouette splayed across the roof of the dormer. His heart sank, but his military experience stood him in good stead. Calmly, but loudly enough to be heard above the rain and wind, Rick said, "Currant, be good enough to fetch a ladder. Quickly, please."

Marianna was thinking about dying. She was wondering how it was going to feel when she hit the ground, just as the rock had, and how long she would lie there in the rain before she was discovered. How much she wished she had never left the assembly! How much she longed to be back there, safe and warm and dry at Rick's side. So strong was her desire to be with him again that she thought she could actually hear his voice calling to her.

And then she saw him and knew she hadn't been dreaming of him, after all. Rick was with her, leaning crazily out the window. His fingers were twined about her ankle like iron, dragging her across the slippery tiles until at last he had pulled her over the sill and into the sitting room. She fell against him, and he caught her, gripping her arms, bruising her skin, drawing her to him.

He was as wet as she was, yet she clung to him as though he was a lifeline, thankful for the hardness of his chest beneath the drenched linen of his shirt. She wanted his comfort, but she wasn't to have it. Instead, she had a taste of his fury as his hands gripped her even harder and he gave her a slight shake.

"Have you completely lost your senses?" he demanded fiercely. "You could have been killed out there!"

It was needless for him to tell her so, for she was vividly aware of the danger she had been in. Even now her knees were trembling so violently, she rather feared that if he let her go, she would dissolve into nothing more than a heap on the floor.

She nodded, afraid to speak, staring down at the tips of Rick's sodden shoes.

"Well?" he said savagely, giving her another slight shake. "Haven't you any explanation?"

"The rain was coming in—no one would help—it seemed such a simple thing—" Like the rest of her, her voice was shaking so much, she couldn't continue. Tears began to prick the backs of her eyes, and she fought bravely against them.

Rick glared down at her, still immersed in anger. He tucked a finger beneath her chin and forced her head back, compelling her to look at him. "I have a good mind to wring your—"

Her eyes blurred; then the tears spilled over.

Halfway between a groan and a curse, he muttered, "Oh, God."

He released her chin, and his other hand relaxed its grip on her shoulders. For a moment he stood there, uncertain, debating the wisdom of giving in to impulse. At last, with a weary sigh, he put his arms around her and drew her close. Gratefully, Marianna rested her cheek against the sodden fabric of his shirt, her body shivering.

She was still enfolded in the circle of his arms when the stamp of running feet sounded in the corridor. Currant appeared in the doorway, out of breath, looking quite alarmed. "Thank heaven!" he breathed at the sight of them. "Is the lady all right, sir?"

"She's safe, thank God," said Rick over the top of her head. "Light a fire in my room, will you, Currant? We've got to get her dry before she catches her death."

Obediently, Currant disappeared. Marianna, too, reacted to Rick's words. Rather, her body reacted: her long-suffering legs, weakened by the shivering spasms that had plagued her since Rick had first dragged her inside, now gave way.

The next thing she knew, she was in Rick's arms, and he was carrying her down the dark corridor. He kicked open a door and carried her inside, to where Currant was coaxing a reluctant fire to life. Rick nudged a small sofa nearer the hearth before depositing Marianna on it.

"Let's get this thing off you," he said, kneeling before her and untying the sodden ribbons of her cape from about her neck. "It's a wonder you haven't been strangled by now."

She chanced a look up at him. There was a grim expression in his eyes as he drew the limp cape from her back and tossed it into a sodden heap on the floor. Clasping her hand, he drew her arm out full-length and began to rub it vigorously.

"Tell me which room is yours and I'll send Currant to fetch you dry clothes."

"He mustn't," she said, through still trembling lips. "He'll wake Blessing."

He stopped rubbing. "Why would she be wakened?"

"Because we share a room."

He was silent a moment, then muttered, "It's just as well." He got up and went to the wardrobe. Drawing a robe and nightshirt from its depths, he dropped them on the sofa beside her. "Here, put these on."

She eyed them bleakly. "But—"

"For God's sake, Marianna, can't you do anything I ask without arguing, just once?"

She took a deep breath. "Yes," she said, in barely a whisper.

She heard the door latch and knew she was alone. She changed out of her wet clothes as quickly as her tired body would allow. Dressed in Rick's nightclothes, shivering from reaction and cold, she awaited his return, not knowing what to expect from him. Her nerves were already raw from her ordeal, and the comfort she had expected from him had been grudgingly given. If he shouted at her again, she didn't think she would be able to bear it.

He returned a few minutes later, having changed into dry clothes—a shirt and waistcoat over comfortable buckskins. He looked down at her and asked calmly, "Feeling better?"

She nodded, unable to trust her voice.

"You're still shivering. You'll have to move nearer the fire if you're going to get warm." He pushed the sofa, with Marianna on it, a bit closer to the hearth and sat down beside her.

He wrapped his arms around her, drawing her against him, lending his warmth to that of the fire. Slowly, feeling began to penetrate her chilled body, giving her the courage to ask, in a voice muffled against his chest, "Are you very angry with me?"

"Yes," he said emphatically. "If the roof needed to be fixed, why didn't you apply to me? Why didn't you—? Don't bother to answer, for I have a fairly good notion what you will say. Mind you, there's no excuse for what you did tonight, Marianna, but I recognize my responsibility in it. We should have settled this dispute between us long ago." He was silent a moment, holding her, stroking the damp ropes of her hair hanging down her back. He said in a quiet voice, "If anything had happened to you—! My God, Marianna, you took a devil of a chance!"

"I'm sorry," she said in a low voice. "I was so frightened. If it hadn't been for you . . ." She dared not finish the thought.

Rick shifted his position slightly and slipped one arm under her legs, lifting her so she lay across him. Then he held her, so closely she could feel the beat of his racing heart against her cheek. It was heaven in his arms, and she didn't care what happened tonight or tomorrow, as long as he held her now.

He said quietly, "I'd say that what you need is a good night's sleep." When she didn't respond, he held her away slightly and looked down at her. "Marianna?"

"Please don't send me away yet," she asked, her fingers clutching at his waistcoat. "Couldn't I just sleep here?"

"Couldn't you just—*what?*" he asked incredulously.

"I won't be any bother to you, I promise!"

Too late, he thought, for she had already bothered him. From the moment he had first seen her, when she launched a pillow at his head, she had bothered him, disturbed his rest, intruded upon his life. And now she wanted to sleep beside him as if such a request were as common as asking him to pass a bowl of pudding at table.

"Marianna, do you know what you are asking?"

"I only know I can't go back to my room. Not yet, at least. Please?" She saw him hesitate, and said bleakly, "I know you think I'm a horrid coward. I'm sorry."

"*You're* sorry," he muttered, almost beneath his breath.

She watched him stare into the fire for a long moment, frowning, as if he were conducting his own quiet internal debate, when the thought occurred to her that he didn't want her there. He didn't want her there, and he couldn't bring himself to tell her so.

Mortified, she set her hands against his chest and pushed herself away. She couldn't bring herself to meet his gaze as she struggled to sit up. "Perhaps I should go, after all," she faltered.

Gently, he pulled her back and held her against the hard muscles of his body. He said rigidly, "The only thing you have to do, Marianna, is go to sleep. And if there's a God in heaven, so will I."

She did sleep and was rather astonished to wake to the gray light of day and the sound of rain pattering against the window. Even before she opened her eyes, she had the odd feeling that she wasn't in her own bed, in her own room; and yet, she wasn't alarmed by that realization. Instead, she felt warm, safe, and infinitely happy. She was rather tempted to just remain where she was, snuggling against the comfortable warmth, heedless of the hour.

Her eyes opened slightly, and she took a cursory stock of her surroundings, of the dark drapes at the window, the massive carved bed against the far wall. She closed her eyes and nestled back against pleasing warmth that was her pillow, knowing that she wasn't in her own room at all, but in Rick's room.

Rick's room! Her eyes flew open. Now thoroughly awake, she realized that she had spent the night in his room, and that delicious warmth, that pleasing comfort she had felt, had come from Rick himself. Her head was against his broad chest, and his arms were about her, one of his hands circling her shoulders, the other at her hip. Together they were lying on the settee, she rather on top of him, their bodies twined together, their clothing in tangles.

Marianna felt a rush of embarrassment and raised herself up on one elbow. She immediately regretted doing so, for his arm fell away from her shoulders, and that feeling of safety and comfort that she had so reveled in but moments before disappeared.

Her eyes flew to his face. Had he awakened? Had he seen her furious blushes and guessed just how shocked she was to find herself in such a position?

He was still asleep, his head resting against the arm of the settee, his tanned throat exposed from where he had loosened his collar. His dark lashes brushed against the high points of his cheeks, and a lock of his hair was lying across his forehead.

Recklessly, she considered settling back down against him, resting her head upon his strong chest and draping his arm once again about her shoulders, but she didn't. Instead, she found herself watching the rhythmic rise of his chest and examining the strong length of his forearms from where he had rolled back the sleeves of his shirt.

She loved him, of that she was certain, and she wondered if there would ever come a time when he might love her just a little. It was futile to tease herself over such a question, especially when she was quite aware that Rick spent a sizable amount of his time with Isabelle. That he preferred the company of her sophisticated, beautiful cousin over hers was the bitterest of pills she had yet been made to swallow. Rashly, she thought that she might very well be persuaded to give up much, including Seven Hills, if only Rick could be made to transfer his affections from Isabelle to her.

That was a startling realization and one that bothered her a great deal, for she had never thought herself of such a romantic turn. Rick Beauleigh was responsible for quite a few changes in her life, she thought, and seemed to wield a greater influence over her emotions than she had appreciated.

Quietly, so as not to disturb him, she untangled herself from Rick and crept from the room. In her own chamber, she dressed and combed the tangles from her hair and tied it with a simple ribbon at the back of her neck.

Downstairs she found Miss Blessington in the kitchens, preparing their morning meal. She was vigorously kneading a pastry dough and looked up as Marianna entered. The look in her eyes was disapproving, and her mouth clamped into a thin line before she said, "There you are, at last. I spent the better part of the night waiting for you to come home, Miss Marianna."

"Don't try to bamboozle me, Blessing," she said, with some amusement, "for I found you fast asleep in your bed last night."

"Which is more than I can say for you. Imagine my shock to wake this morning and find you hadn't been to bed. I dare not think where you spent the night, Miss Marianna, but I do recall—very well, too!—that you're a young lady who was never raised to behave so! When I remember your dear parents and how carefully they raised you—!"

"Blessing, stop!" cried Marianna in horror. "You cannot believe—how could you even *think* that I would be capable of such things as you have imagined! I assure you, I have done nothing to cause you such concern. Why, last night I merely—" She stopped short, not at all certain how to proceed.

Last night I merely spent the night in Rick's room. Last night I merely slept with Rick. No matter how she phrased the explanation in her mind, it didn't at all sound as innocent as it should have.

She said, quite earnestly, "Dearest Blessing, you must believe that I did nothing to cause you such heartache. I shall give you an explanation if you will have it."

Miss Blessington gave a final, vigorous jab at the bread

dough. "Very well, Miss Marianna. I shall listen to whatever you have to tell me."

"I don't know which is worse, Blessing: to know you think me capable of acting as less than a lady, or to have you think me foolish. For you shall think just so after I have told you what I did last night. I got very angry, you see—perhaps even a trifle jealous," she admitted reluctantly. "I simply couldn't bear to see Mr. Beauleigh and Isabelle together, and when Isabelle told me that he came from a very grand family and was terribly wealthy, I immediately believed the worst of him."

"How, child, can you believe the worst of a man who has been so kind to you?"

"I don't know," she said, feeling wretched, indeed. "But why would he hide from us all manner of information concerning his family and his history? Why, he even speaks French—and fluently, too! Why would he deceive me, Blessing? Why would he wish me to believe he needed lessons, if not to make me appear foolish?"

"There was no harm done, child, but I don't think you're willing to see that right now. And I daresay Mr. Beauleigh might have told you anything you wished to know, if only you would have asked. Instead, your cousin felt she had the right to speak on his behalf."

"But that's not the worst of it, Blessing, for I behaved very badly after Isabelle told me about Mr. Beauleigh," Marianna said in a rush. "I left the assembly, without a word to anyone, even Mr. Beauleigh, and came home alone. I was angry and did something so foolish—I cannot speak of it, even to you. I was in a horrid fix, and Mr. Beauleigh came to my assistance. I was upset, and he was kind to me and let me pass the night on the sofa in his room. But nothing else occurred, I assure you." She searched the face of her old nurse for some sign of understanding. "You do believe me, don't you, Blessing?"

"Of course I do, child, but you gave me quite a scare. I've spent so many years looking after you, I must be forgiven if I worry about you." She hesitated a moment, then said, in a much gentler voice, "And how, exactly, was Mr. Beauleigh kind to you last night, child?"

At first Marianna didn't understand fully what Miss Blessington was asking, but after a dawning moment, a hot, guilty flush covered her cheeks. "He simply—" She faltered, and was unable for a moment to meet the older woman's gaze. Too easily did she recall how it felt to wake up next to him that morning, to know that she had slept so peacefully within the circle of his arms, and to know, too, that if she ever had the chance to do so again, she would not hesitate. But she couldn't very well admit such thoughts to her nurse, and said slowly, "He simply comforted me, Blessing, much as an older brother would do."

No sooner did those words leave her lips, than she realized she had spoken nothing but the truth. Rick had behaved very much as an older brother last night, ordering her about, scolding her, and wishing her otherwhere than in his room. While she had reveled in the feel of his strong arms about her, he had held himself in rigid check, and when she had asked to remain with him, he had clearly not wanted her there.

It was a horrid thing to realize that she was in love with a man who did not love her in return, and up until that moment, she had never felt the full impact of it. But now she felt utterly alone, unable even to confide in Miss Blessington, her oldest and most trusted friend.

Fifteen

"No French lessons today, Marianna?"

Marianna almost jumped. She was sitting at her writing table in the blue sitting room, scribbling a bit of prose, and had not perceived Rick's presence in the doorway. She looked up to find him standing there, quite at his ease, looking remarkably handsome and achingly masculine. She had to force herself to divert her eyes back to the sheet of paper before her. "I do not think, Mr. Beauleigh, that someone as fluent as you are in other languages could possibly be in need of any further lessons."

"And what," he asked, as he sauntered into the room, "makes you think I am fluent in other languages?"

"Certainly, *I* had no notion, but my cousin, Isabelle, put me in mind of it last night. She mentioned that your talents aren't limited to French—you also speak Italian and Spanish, it seems."

He was quiet for a moment. "Is that what set you off last night?"

"Set me off? Not at all, but it did cause me to wonder why you deceived me into thinking you spoke no other language and needed me to teach you. It was a horrid trick, Mr. Beauleigh."

"I don't think so. After all, you got what you wanted: a paying pupil."

"And how did you benefit from the arrangement? What did you get?"

"I got to spend some time with you."

She looked quickly up at him, half-afraid she had not heard him right. "Th-that was a benefit?"

"Indeed it was, for it was the only means I could contrive to speak with you without your nurse or brother in attendance. You've no notion, I think, how much they rely upon you."

She felt herself blushing, but said, "We have spoken without interruption on other occasions—at dinner, for instance."

He cast her a speaking look that caused her blushes to reappear.

"*You* contrived that we should dine alone? How did you ever compel Blessing to agree to such a scheme?"

"She only wants what is best for you, and it took little effort on my part to persuade her that young ladies of breeding do not take their meals in kitchens."

She didn't know what to think or say. She was certainly flattered and more than a little flustered to realize that he was more strongly attracted to her than she had given him credit. And when he leaned across the writing table and placed his warm hand over her fingers and said compellingly, "Dine with me again tonight?" she could do no more than nod her head in, as she later reflected, a fashion that was much too vigorous to be seemly.

No sooner did he leave, than she realized that she had been breathing quite unsteadily and that her heart was thumping ridiculously against her ribs. She had not known that love could exact such a physical response. It was a long time before she redirected her attention to the page of prose before her, and longer still before she could comprehend the words that she had written. She preferred to spend her time recounting the words Rick had spoken to her and the manner in which he had said them. Everything he had ever said to her, every one of his actions where she was concerned, now took on a different meaning. What she had once seen as his intrusion in her life, she now saw as an example of his kindness. Where she had once scolded him for interfering with her family, she now saw his actions as an illustration of his affection for Robin and Miss Blessington. Certainly, he had been kind to Jemmy, and it was only her own stubbornness that had kept him from easing some of the burden from her shoulders. In a very short time she realized that she had once again been reduced to the state of a romantic schoolgirl. But this time, she didn't mind one bit.

Marianna could not resist an impulse to go out to the stables that afternoon, and she did so on the merest of pretexts. She told herself that she wished only to make certain that Jemmy and Robin were behaving themselves and not making a nuisance with the horses, but in truth, she longed for another glimpse of Rick.

She found Robin near the paddock. Nearby, Currant was teaching Jemmy the proper way in which to harness a horse to a gig. Robin greeted her happily, saying, "Only fancy all the things Jemmy is learning, Marianna. And after he's finished, he promised to teach me what Currant has taught him."

"That sounds a most satisfactory arrangement. Jemmy is a good friend to you."

"He's my *best* friend," said Robin decisively. "Sometimes I think Jemmy is like my brother, since I don't have one. He likes living here at Seven Hills, and so do I."

Marianna's heart sank a little. She said gently, "Robin, what would you think if we had to leave Seven Hills?"

"Why would we, Marianna? We're happy here and so

much better off than we were in that horrid little tenant cottage we lived in before. Why would we leave?"

"It's rather difficult to explain, but it may turn out that Seven Hills doesn't belong to us, after all."

"Who does it belong to, then?" he demanded.

"It may happen that Seven Hills belongs to Mr. Beauleigh."

"Then, we have nothing to worry about, I should think. Mr. Beauleigh will let us live here, just as he lets Jemmy live here. And he knows, too, that Jemmy and I won't be separated. We're best of friends, Marianna."

"Yes, but sometimes things occur that we cannot control. Sometimes we must leave a place we love."

"We won't be leaving Seven Hills," Robin protested. "And I won't go anywhere Jemmy doesn't go."

She was a little surprised by his reaction and decided to say no more. She returned to the house and helped Miss Blessington in the kitchen, but she gave a great deal of thought to what Robin had said.

John Bagwell arrived late that afternoon, and his visit provided Marianna with a welcome diversion.

"I cannot stay," he said, as he followed her into the drawing room, "but I do have a matter of importance to discuss with Beauleigh."

"That is too bad, Mr. Bagwell. I was rather hoping you had come with news of Seven Hills. It seems such a long time since we first began our dispute over the place."

"Has it been difficult for you? You may speak frankly with me, you know, for I've known Rick Beauleigh for many years and am well acquainted with his more difficult side."

"It hasn't been easy," she said, carefully choosing her words, "but we are going on together much better now."

"I'm glad of it, for I shouldn't like to see you unhappy." After a short pause, he asked gently, "Has Rick ever made you unhappy? No, you needn't answer, for I have seen it in your eyes on more than one occasion. You have a very expressive face, Miss Madison, and I think I would not be far off the mark to think that there have been times when our Mr. Beauleigh has made you very unhappy indeed. Last evening, for instance?"

She couldn't have been more shocked and looked at him quickly, wondering how he had gauged her emotions so well, when she had taken such pains to escape the assembly before anyone could guess her state of mind.

"Just so!" said Mr. Bagwell, a little triumphantly. "You see, I know you much better than you might allow. I also know Rick. He would never listen to me were I to voice my objections over his alliance with your cousin."

"His alliance?" she asked, in an odd tone.

"Surely you knew! Rick was always quite candid that he intended to court Isabelle Madison in hopes she might influence her uncle, for he thought by doing so, Cecil Madison would retract his bequest to you. And while his plan hasn't yet worked as he expected, I believe he has found an excellent match in Isabelle."

"An excellent match?" she repeated rigidly.

"Miss Madison, I thought you knew all this," he said, looking very much concerned. "But I can see now you did not. Oh, wicked Rick Beauleigh! He left you quite unsuspecting, didn't he? I shall curse him if he promised you marriage, for he's never been the marrying kind and never shall be!"

Unsure what to think, not knowing what to believe, Marianna could do no more than shake her head. "No! I mean, yes, I was unsuspecting, but—! Oh, there must be some mistake!"

"There's no mistake, I fear. If it's any comfort to you, Miss Madison, you are not the first young lady to mistake the intent behind his charm."

Comfort! She would never feel comfort again, she thought. How could she be so much in love with Rick Beauleigh one moment, and so mistrustful of him the next? In truth, she knew very little about him, and she had had reason in the past to doubt his motives. Why, she had even suspected in the past that he might attempt to beguile her into giving up her claim to Seven Hills. But now, for his best friend to present her with evidence of such a deed was quite past bearing.

Mr. Bagwell took her hand. "I've shocked you. I'm sorry! I didn't mean to distress you, Miss Madison— Marianna!"

With her hand in his, it was a simple task for him to pull her a little to him, and before she even realized it, she found that she was in his arms. She thought at first he meant to comfort her, much as a brother might console a sister, but no sooner did his arms snake about her, than she felt a small flicker of alarm. She stiffened slightly, but he didn't seem to notice.

"He did flirt with you, didn't he?" he asked softly. "And he charmed you quite thoroughly, I should think. How foolish you were! For you must have known that your efforts would have been much more to the point and to your greater advantage had you expended them on me."

She didn't have the slightest idea what he was talking about, but she knew that she didn't wish to be held so. She gave an ineffectual push against his chest. "Mr. Bagwell—!"

"You mustn't think you need to play the innocent maid with me, for you see, I know all about your rather intimate arrangement with Rick Beauleigh."

"My—my arrangement?" she repeated, staring up at him.

"The very same arrangement I hope you will strike

with me. I daresay that I may not be as generous as Rick, for I'm not as plump in the pocket as he, but I assure you, I might be persuaded to award Seven Hills and much more to you if you please me."

Before she could make sense of these bewildering words, Marianna found herself being kissed. She fought strenuously to break free from his hold, but her efforts only made Mr. Bagwell hold her tighter.

"Mr. Bagwell, *please!*" she cried, and suddenly found that she was no longer struggling against an amorous solicitor. Mr. Bagwell was sprawled upon the floor, a startled look upon his face, a patch of pink upon his chin, and Rick was standing over him.

"Good God, Rick!" he exclaimed from his position on the carpet. "What did you do that for?"

"You cannot think to treat a lady in such a fashion without some repercussion."

"A lady?" Mr. Bagwell repeated. "Marianna Madison? Rick, you cannot mean it!"

His blue eyes narrowed. "Do me the favor of getting up, will you, so I may knock you down again!"

"Here, now, what has got into you?" demanded Mr. Bagwell, scrambling quickly to his feet and backing swiftly out of reach. "You're kicking up an awful fuss over a simple kiss. It was nothing more, and no real harm was done. I daresay it's nothing she hasn't endured before!"

Rick took a step toward him, his fists clenched, and a furious curl to his lips.

"Get out!" Rick ordered, and he didn't find the need to repeat the command a second time. The door slammed shut behind Mr. Bagwell. A moment later, his step was heard on the drive outside, and in another moment, the crunch of his carriage wheels against the drive sounded through the open window.

A sudden feeling of cold engulfed Marianna. Shivering, she wrapped her slim arms about herself, her body tense, her eyes seeking out anything of comfort in the room. She could feel Rick's gaze upon her, and she looked up at him. There was a look there she had never seen before, and she didn't know if she should be frightened or trusting of it. She knew only that she was mortified and in dire need of comfort—and there was no one to offer her any. She cast Rick a distracted look and tried to marshal her self-control.

"What just happened here, Marianna?" he asked patiently.

"Nothing. Nothing at all," she answered, fighting the impulse to wring her hands. "Mr. Bagwell simply called—he said he had some business to discuss with you."

"What sort of business? Or should I naturally assume the only business John Bagwell has to discuss is the ownership of Seven Hills?"

"He said he could ensure the place would come to me if only I—" She stopped, unwilling to repeat those hateful words.

"If only what, Marianna?" he asked, frowning. He waited patiently for her to continue, and it took a few moments for him to realize that he might find himself waiting in vain.

At last she uttered, in a voice that was barely audible, "He said that you weren't the kind of man who marries . . ." Her voice trailed away in a tide of embarrassment.

Rick drew a deep breath, and muttered wearily, "Oh my God."

How he crossed the room so quickly, she had no notion, for it seemed he had only to take a single step before she found herself engulfed in his arms. His hands claimed her, pressing her against him, holding her tightly, reassuringly. Wonderfully.

"He didn't hurt you, did he?" he asked after a moment.

She didn't wish to say or do anything that might break the spell and cause him to take his strong arms away. At last she said, in a voice muffled against his lapel, "No, he didn't hurt me, but he was horrid just the same."

"I won't apologize for his behavior, but I cannot think what possessed him to act so. I've known John for years and never knew him the cur."

After a long, painful moment of recollection, she said, "I think I know what possessed him. Those things he said—those hateful, horrid things!—about your living here—" She stopped, not at all certain she wished to continue. "Blessing thought the same thing. When she discovered I hadn't been to bed, she—she thought the worst."

Rick frowned. "It doesn't sound like Miss Blessington to be of such a suspicious turn. Do you think it would do any good if I spoke to her?"

"No, for I think she believed me when I explained what happened, but the damage was already done, you see. She had already leapt to the wrong conclusion. Why must people be so quick to think the worst? Why cannot people believe that you and I live in the same house simply because circumstances dictate we must?"

He didn't know what to say, but he sensed she was in desperate need of comfort. His arms tightened a little. "I wish I could give you an answer, Marianna."

"You warned me this would happen," she said, rather forlornly. "I should have listened to you."

"*I* warned you?" he asked, surprised.

"Yes, when you first came to Seven Hills. You told me the neighbors would judge me if I remained. You warned me I would be labeled a scarlet woman."

He had long forgotten having uttered that petty predic-
tion, and he was a little startled that she would recall his
words with such clarity. "Marianna, when I said that to
you—"

"You were right, of course, and how I wish I had listened to you! But it's too late now, isn't it?" She was
quiet a moment; then she asked, rather piteously, "Is my
reputation entirely in ruins?"

For the first time in a long while, Rick Beauleigh found
himself at a loss for words. No comforting maxims
sprang to his mind. He could think of nothing he might
say that would erase the expression of utter misery from
Marianna's lovely face.

When he didn't speak, she let out a groan of frustration. "It is all so unfair! Why must I—I, who have done
nothing wrong!—be judged so harshly, while my cousin,
Isabelle, throws herself at men without the least censure?
It is a great inequity!"

He couldn't help but smile at her logic. "It is, indeed.
If it is any measure of comfort to you, I doubt very much
that your cousin ever incited the same passionate outburst
in a man as you did in John Bagwell."

"*That* is a distinction I would gladly forego! How horrid he was! I shall not endure being kissed a second time,
I assure you!"

She felt Rick's body go rigid against hers, and after a
moment he said, rather incredulously, "A second time?
Are you telling me you had your first kiss just now from
John Bagwell? Marianna, you had never been kissed before?"

"Never, and I daresay if all kisses are the same as the
one I was just made to suffer, I heartily hope I shall never
be kissed again!"

There was a moment of silence. Then, astonishingly,
she heard him laugh softly. He tightened his arms about

her, pressing her against him, until she could feel the rumbling vibration of his laughter through his chest.

After a moment, he said gently, "Marianna, if you were kissed correctly, believe me, you would want to be kissed again."

"I don't believe it," she said, giving her head a slight shake. She thought of John Bagwell's harsh lips on hers, of his invasive mouth and his clumsy hands at her waist. She almost shivered. "Kissing is a horrid business! I—I shall never be kissed again!"

"Are you sure, Marianna?" he murmured. "You should be very certain before you make any rash judgments."

There was something rather tantalizing in his tone, and she looked up at him. Their eyes met, her eyes wide with questions, his dark with purpose and some other emotion she couldn't quite bring herself to name. Whatever caused that look, it was certainly hypnotic, for she found that she couldn't look away. Even when he adjusted his hold of her, sliding one hand around her waist to fold her more tightly against him, she remained yielding and compliant in his arms, mesmerized by what she saw in his expression. And when she suddenly realized that his handsome face was slowly nearing hers, she was powerless to do anything about it.

His firm lips brushed against the astonished softness of her own. His kiss was so light, so fleeting, that she was filled with disappointment that it hadn't lasted longer. She opened her eyes and saw that Rick was looking down at her, gauging her reaction. Then he lowered his head and claimed her lips in a long, sensual caress.

Rick was right, Marianna thought dazedly. Kisses were like heaven when they were given correctly. And Rick's kisses were of the glorious, drugging variety that had the power to make her forget everything but the wonder of his embrace.

After a few moments he lifted his head and stared own at her shining gray eyes. He took the time to regain ne mastery of himself and said, "Now you have a basis or comparison, Marianna. Can you tell the difference etween my kisses and John Bagwell's? And, mind you, shall know if you are telling me less than the truth."

"I could never lie about such a thing," she murmured nrough a happy fog. And then she surprised herself by aying brazenly, "Mr. Beauleigh, will you please kiss me gain?"

Sixteen

For the past three weeks, Rick Beauleigh had been behaving like an idiot. It was a hard fact to face, and one he didn't at all care to admit, but it was a truth he could no longer ignore. He was an idiot. Only an idiot, he reasoned, would spend his days mooning over a woman he barely knew, involving himself in her personal struggles and going well out of his way to please her when she had given no indication at all that she appreciated his efforts. He wasn't used to being treated so. After all, he was Rick Beauleigh, the hero of the Peninsular Wars, the most favored son of a wealthy and powerful family. People didn't tell him what to do—he told them, and almost without exception he got what he wanted. Yet in the last three weeks, he had found himself behaving more like a lovesick schoolboy than a confident, decisive man of twenty-eight years. He should have been telling Marianna what to do and how to do it; instead, she had been making his decisions for him. How else could he explain that his groom—a man sought after for his skill and revered by many as one of England's foremost experts in horseflesh—was spending his days toiling away at household chores? And how else could he account for the fact that he spent every afternoon pretending to learn French or chasing after two inquisitive boys who should have been in school instead of haunting his stables? He had come

Seven Hills seeking quiet and peace, a haven away
om the pressures of his family and any reminders of
e war and the havoc it had wreaked upon his body.
stead, he had found Marianna Madison, and the serenity
r which he had wished had never materialized.

Or had it? He certainly felt at peace lolling on a blanket
neath the gnarled branches of an oak tree, listening to
arianna recite French exercises in her sweet, soothing
ice. And he had most assuredly experienced a certain
renity while spending an evening in the company of a
ving family, as they played games or read aloud to each
ther. He had always thought he would find happiness in
solitary existence, but he had come to realize that he
ad been wrong about that, too. His perception of the
orld had changed drastically over the course of the last
w weeks, and he now believed he would find happiness
nly with Marianna Madison. It was an unfortunate co-
cidence that she hadn't seemed to share that sentiment.

Until now. As she stood within the circle of his arms,
er lips raised invitingly toward his, it was all he could
o not to crush her to him and claim her mouth in a
emanding kiss. When she looked up at him, with her
ps half-parted and her gray eyes alight with passion, he
new it would take a great effort on his part to control
e moment, but control it, he would. Between the two
f them, he would have to be the sensible one. Slowly,
luctantly, he loosened his hold about her.

"I think it's time you and I had a talk."

She didn't want to talk. She wanted to be kissed and
as on the verge of telling him so in no uncertain terms,
hen she saw the look of determination in his eyes. She
sked warily, "What do you want to talk about?"

"Seven Hills. You. Us."

Now? Couldn't he have picked a different time to speak
f such things? She felt his hands slipping away from her

waist, and a strong feeling of disappointment swept ov
her. "Very well," she said, steeling herself against wha
ever he had to say.

"Come here and sit down. I've been thinking, and I'v
come to the conclusion that we cannot continue on as v
have been. It isn't right that we live together in the san
house. Your experience with John Bagwell illustrated th
argument only too well!" He waited for her to say som
thing, and when she didn't, he mistook her silence fe
agreement. "I suggest we would be better off to sett
this matter between ourselves."

He sounded so purposeful, so determined, that sh
longed for him to speak to her in the same soft, mee
merizing tone he had used when he had held her in h
arms. How did he come to have such strong will? Wha
had occurred in his life to cause the momentary dark
ness she had glimpsed behind the clear blue of his eyes
All along he had alternately intrigued and teased he
and the many questions she had about him disturbe
her greatly. Suddenly, before she could stop herself, sh
asked, "Why do you want Seven Hills so much? Wh
out of all the estates and grand homes in England, mus
you have just this one?"

He seemed momentarily taken aback. "Why do yo
ask?"

"It's a fair question, Mr. Beauleigh. You know the rea
sons I must have Seven Hills. Suppose you tell me wh
you are so determined to own it, as well." When he didn
answer right away, she said, "Do you wish to live at Seve
Hills because you lived here as a child?"

"To a certain extent."

"You told me you were happy here. Is that why?"

"Partially. It's not an exciting story, Marianna."

"Tell me anyway," she said coaxingly.

"The days I spent at Seven Hills were the only day

I was happy. My mother and father were not like yours, Marianna. They married not for love, but because they were destined to by their parents. I was raised not by a doting mother and father, as you were, but by parents who were so miserably unhappy with their lot in life, they never realized how unhappy they made those around them."

"I'm sorry," she said gently. "That must have been very difficult to grow up in such an atmosphere."

"It was. But here, at Seven Hills, I was happy. My aunt saw to that. I always equated this place with peace and joy and contentment. Even when I was with my regiment, I would think of Seven Hills and knew that I would return to this place one day." He had never before opened his soul to anyone. He had certainly never bared the secrets hidden away in his heart. It was too difficult to tell anyone that he had been an unwanted child, living virtually alone in a vast, museumlike estate with parents who had no time for him.

"And so you have returned. But instead of finding peace and solitude, you found me and my troubles. Oh, Rick, why didn't you ever tell me? All this time I thought you wanted Seven Hills merely because of some whim to possess it. I'm glad you told me the real reason at last."

"Does it make a difference?"

"Yes. It does to me." She was silent a moment, trying to envision Rick as a boy, roaming the echoing corridors of an enormous house, growing up without the love of a mother and father. "Perhaps you do have the prior claim, after all."

A strange light leapt in the depths of his eyes. "Indeed? Do you mean to tell me you would give up your right to Seven Hills?"

She nodded slightly, unable to understand why he was

staring at her so. "Now that I know how much it means to you, I couldn't possibly insist upon having the place as my own, could I?"

He let loose a deep sigh, as if he had been holding his breath. "My dearest girl!"

In the next moment, Marianna found herself once again enveloped within the sweet embrace of Rick's arms. Although she was very happy, indeed, to find herself so, she wasn't at all sure why he had so suddenly felt compelled to hold her.

"Mr. Beauleigh—!"

"Rick. My name is Rick, and I should like nothing more than to hear my name on those sweet lips of yours."

She obliged him, and said shyly, "Rick—only tell me what is happening."

"Gladly. You see, I've fallen in love with a very stubborn young woman, who shall no doubt plague me day and night with problems and worries."

She looked up at him, a light of hope in her eyes, and meekly asked, "Is it me?"

"It is, indeed. I think I've loved you from the moment you threw that ridiculous pillow at my head, and I haven't stopped. I've loved you with mud on your skirt, and I've loved you when you were soaking wet. I would have spoken to you before this, but I couldn't be certain of your feelings—until you offered to give up your claim to Seven Hills for me. Then I was sure you felt some affection for me, too. You do love me, don't you, Marianna?"

There was no use denying it. "Yes. I do love you, Rick."

He smiled triumphantly, happily, and kissed her lightly upon the mouth. "It seems I've been waiting forever to hear you say that. And by so saying, you've solved the problem of who shall live at Seven Hills. We both shall, if you agree to marry me."

She said, a little faintly, "I can think of nothing I want more."

He could think of no better reward for such a perfect reply than to bestow upon her another kiss, but just as his lips were about to meet hers, she turned her head, crying, "Isabelle!"

"What of her?"

"All this time you've been paying court to her, driving her about the countryside—"

"Enduring her relentless chattering about her family's social position," he finished helpfully. "There was never any understanding between your cousin and me—except that we both knew very well we were using one another. Your cousin hoped I would, at the very least, provide her with some entree into the elite of London Society."

"And what did you use Isabelle for?" she asked suspiciously.

"To make you jealous. I have a feeling it worked."

That was one admission Marianna was unwilling to make, and was saved the trouble of having to do so only because Rick was no longer able to resist temptation and chose that moment to kiss her quite thoroughly.

A few minutes later, after Rick had released her and her fluttering heart had calmed to a sufficient degree, she said, "Shall I tell Blessing?"

"I think we should tell her together, and Robin, too. Do you think they'll like the idea of our being married?"

Marianna rather thought they would be cast into transports over the notion, but was content, instead, to simply lead the way down the corridor in search of Miss Blessington.

They found her alone in the kitchens, sipping a cup of tea. She greeted Marianna and Rick in a rather gruff manner, which didn't soften when Marianna said, "We have some news to tell you, Blessing. I think you shall be pleased to hear it."

"You mustn't think you must tell me anything, Miss Marianna," she said acidly. "After all, I'm simply a servant when all's said and done, for all I have been treated with affection in the past."

"Blessing, is something wrong?" Marianna asked in some exasperation.

Her old nurse took her time in answering. "Not wrong, I should say, but not right, either. I must admit, I'm an old woman, and forgetful of a great many things, but I dare swear I can't remember a time when I've been made to feel as useless as I have today!"

"Dearest Blessing, what *are* you talking about?"

"I'm speaking of Master Robin. I daresay you know what's best for him, but I haven't been biding my time these years where he's concerned. He's in my charge, after all."

Rick interrupted her, saying with authority, "Miss Blessington, has something happened to Robin?"

"He's gone off. I told him not to, but he wouldn't listen to me."

"Gone where, Miss Blessington?"

"He wouldn't say, but I shouldn't have to guess where a boy who is quite horse-mad might go."

"I'll harness the curricle," said Rick, and he left through the back door.

"Blessing, you must tell me what happened and anything you can remember."

With a mulish angle to her chin, Miss Blessington said, "Master Robin asked if he might go into Newmarket to the race courses with Jemmy. I told him no, but when he insisted, I left it to you. 'You must ask your sister,' said I, never dreaming you would go against me in such a matter."

"But, Blessing, Robin never asked me if he could go to Newmarket or anywhere else. Indeed, I haven't spoken to him since I left him at the paddock earlier this afternoon."

"It's not like Master Robin to lie. Whatever possessed him?"

Marianna didn't know, but she was determined to find out. She went out to where Rick was impatiently waiting for Currant to finish harnessing his horses to the curricle. "I'm coming with you," she said, expecting no argument.

He gave her none, but helped her climb up onto the seat. "Jemmy is gone, too. What do you think they mean by it?" he asked, as Currant sprang away from the horses. With a flick of the reins, they were away, bowling down the drive at a tremendous speed.

"Where do you suppose they've gone?" she asked, as she clutched at the side of her seat.

"To Newmarket, if I know your brother. They couldn't have got far."

He was right to think so, for they came upon Robin and Jemmy walking down the road, less than a mile from the house. Rick pulled the curricle up beside them and looked down to see that they were each carrying a valise.

"What's this, Robin?"

Robin looked up at him, a stubborn set to his chin. "Jemmy and I have decided to leave Seven Hills. We're going to Newmarket to earn our own way."

Marianna gasped slightly. "Robin! You cannot be serious!"

"We are, and we won't be dissuaded. Jemmy and I have made up our minds. We won't be separated, Marianna."

"Who said anything about separating the two of you?" Rick asked.

"Marianna did," he said burningly.

She felt the discomfort of knowing that three pairs of eyes were directed at her. "It's true, I talked to Robin earlier today and told him we might have to leave Seven Hills. But the situation has changed, Robin, dear. We won't be leaving."

He looked up at her with a wary expression, then turned his gaze toward Rick. "Is that true, sir? May we stay at Seven Hills, even if it turns out the place belongs to you?"

"It's true, although I cannot decide if I wish to share my home with a scalawag such as you."

Robin smiled up at him. "Then, if you are quite certain, Jemmy and I shall return, after all."

He made a move to scramble up in the curricle, but Rick forestalled him with a gesture. "Not so fast, young man. You and Jemmy shall walk back to the house. That's your punishment for having caused your sister and nurse a good deal of worry."

"But we've already walked so far," he protested. "Why may we not ride back with you?"

"Because I cannot kiss your sister with two boys in the carriage with me," Rick responded promptly.

He then executed a perfect three-point turn in the middle of the road and headed back down the road toward Seven Hills. As soon as he was satisfied they had traveled a sufficient distance to hide their vehicle from the curious eyes of two ten-year-old boys, he brought the curricle to a stop.

Marianna blushed deeply. "Rick Beauleigh! You cannot mean to kiss me in the middle of a public road!"

"I promised your brother I would kiss you," he said masterfully, "and I'm a man who always keeps his promises." Then he slipped one arm about her shoulders and drew her to him, and he proceeded to kiss her, just as he had promised.

More Zebra Regency Romances

__A Noble Pursuit by Sara Blayne $4.99US/$6.50CAN
    0-8217-5756-3

__Crossed Quills by Carola Dunn $4.99US/$6.50CAN
    0-8217-6007-6

__A Poet's Kiss by Valerie King $4.99US/$6.50CAN
    0-8217-5789-X

__Exquisite by Joan Overfield $5.99US/$7.50CAN
    0-8217-5894-2

__The Reluctant Lord by Teresa Desjardien $4.99US/$6.50CAN
    0-8217-5646-X

__A Dangerous Affair by Mona Gedney $4.50US/$5.50CAN
    0-8217-5294-4

__Love's Masquerade by Violet Hamilton $4.99US/$6.50CAN
    0-8217-5409-2

__Rake's Gambit by Meg-Lynn Roberts $4.99US/$6.50CAN
    0-8217-5687-7

__Cupid's Challenge by Jeanne Savery $4.50US/$5.50CAN
    0-8217-5240-5

__A Deceptive Bequest by Olivia Sumner $4.50US/$5.50CAN
    0-8217-5380-0

__A Taste for Love by Donna Bell $4.99US/$6.50CAN
    0-8217-6104-8

Call toll free **1-888-345-BOOK** to order by phone or use this
coupon to order by mail.
Name_____
Address_____
City _____ State _____Zip_____
Please send me the books I have checked above.
I am enclosing $_____
Plus postage and handling* $_____
Sales tax (in New York and Tennessee only) $_____
Total amount enclosed $_____
*Add $2.50 for the first book and $.50 for each additional book.
Send check or money order (no cash or CODs) to:
Kensington Publishing Corp., 850 Third Avenue, New York, NY 10022
Prices and Numbers subject to change without notice.
All orders subject to availability.
Check out our website at **www.kensingtonbooks.com**